Phebe A. Hanaford

The heart of Siasconset

Phebe A. Hanaford

The heart of Siasconset

ISBN/EAN: 9783744737067

Printed in Europe, USA, Canada, Australia, Japan

Cover: Foto ©Andreas Hilbeck / pixelio.de

More available books at **www.hansebooks.com**

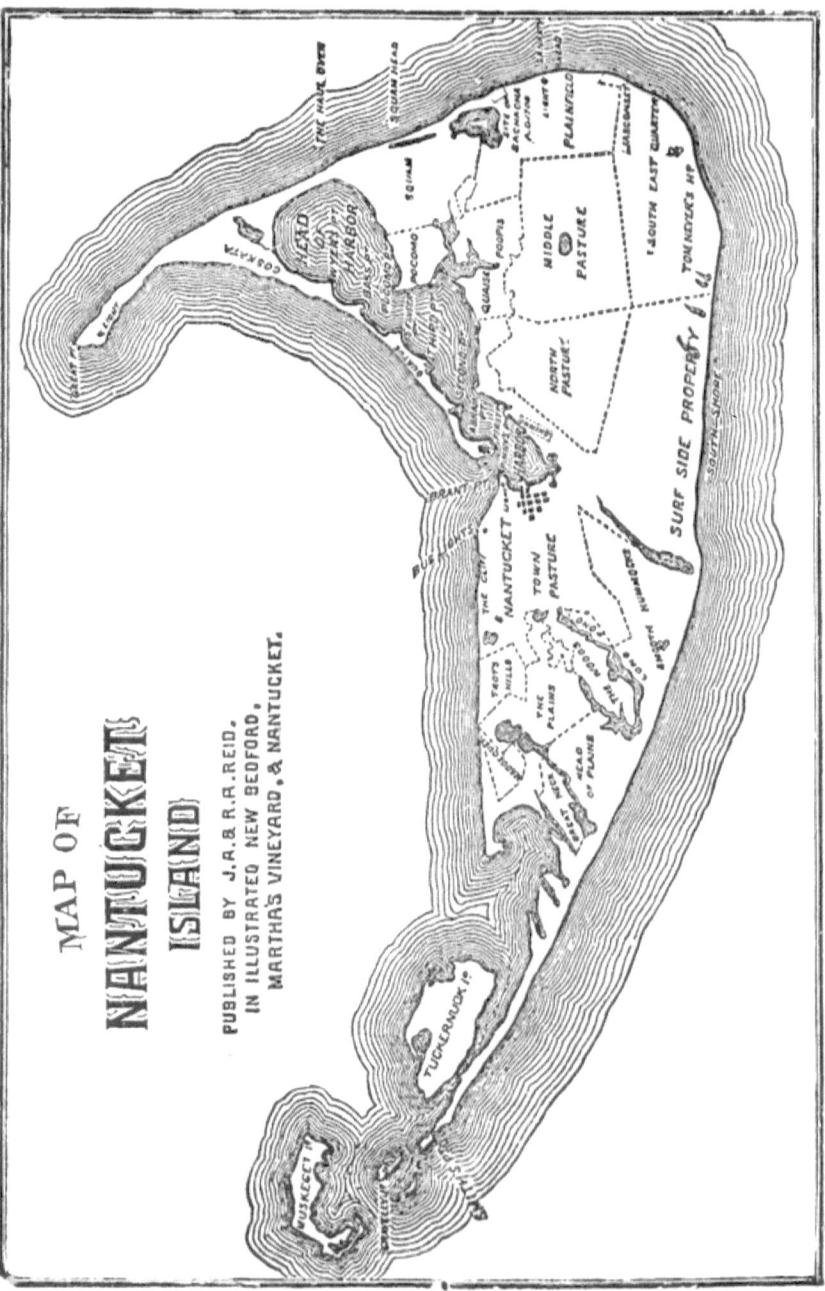

MAP OF
NANTUCKET
ISLAND

PUBLISHED BY J. A. & R. A. REID.
IN ILLUSTRATED NEW BEDFORD,
MARTHA'S VINEYARD, & NANTUCKET.

The

Heart of Siasconset.

BY

Rev. Phebe A. Hanaford,

AUTHOR OF

"Daughters of America, or Women of The Century," Lives of
Peabody, Lincoln and Dickens, "From Shore to Shore
and Other Poems," The Soldier's Daughter," "The
Captive Boy in Terra Del Fuego," "Field,
Gunboat, Hospital and Prison," Lucretia
the Quakeress, etc., etc., etc.

———◦———

The isles shall wait for His law.—Isa. xlii: 4.

Attuned to praise be every voice,
Let not one heart be sad,
Jehovah reigns! Let earth rejoice,
Let all the isles be glad!—M. Rayner.

———◦———

New Haven, Conn. :

PRESS OF HOGGSON & ROBINSON.

1890.

CONTENTS.

ILLUSTRATIONS.

PREFACE.

THIS book is for all those who love Nantucket, and especially for those who enjoy 'Sconset. Its local coloring is high, for it could not be otherwise. Personal allusions are unavoidable in such a book, though it may bring the charge of egotism also to the author. But if the little, sketchy volume shall convey any historical or genealogical knowledge to any reader, and especially if it shall contribute to the happiness of any invalid— thereby helping toward health—I shall be glad that I yielded to the wishes of dear friends, and put pen to paper, in depicting 'Sconset as it is, and the heart of 'Sconset as it always was, and, I hope, always will be.

I am pleased to dedicate it to one who prizes her Nantucket ancestry, though not of island birth herself, and who enjoys those 'Sconset characteristics which are promotive of health, and comfort, and peace.

The illustrations are not numerous, but they are, in my view, valuable. Sancoty has never been better shown, in any engraving, and I am grateful to Harper & Bros. for such a representation of the lighthouse as it was when the " N. M." visited it with the two sisters.

The picture of 'Sconset bluff and beach is all the more valuable to me, because photographed, probably, when my now deceased father was gazing on the ocean through his spy-glass.

The map is valuable as showing the shape of the Island, and the locality of 'Sconset thereupon. From the firm of J. A. & R. A. Reed of Providence were obtained for this book the map and the 'Sconset picture, and I have gladly availed myself of these illustrations, feeling sure they enhance the value, though they do not increase the price, of

"THE HEART OF SIASCONSET."

(The title was original with "Helen.")

Hoping that many of my friends, far and near, w enjoy this descriptive narration of life "on 'Scon Bank," and "strangers" will be led by it to find heal and comfort upon this historic island,

"I launch my venture on an untried sea."

THE AUTHOR.

539 Howard Avenue,
    NEW HAVEN, CONN.

HEART OF SIASCONSET.

CHAPTER I.

REST FOR THE WEARY.

"But come to that island each brother in feeling,
    And ye who can call it your birthplace and home ;
Away from vexation and vanity stealing
    To purity, peace and simplicity come."

HENRY GLOVER.

COME away from the bustle and heat of the city, will you ?" exclaimed Helen to her sister, Jean. "You are weary with your long years of teaching and you need a restful change."

"No doubt of that, sister," was the reply, "but where shall I go ? I have tried Niagara and the White Mountains and Europe. They all refreshed me for a

season, but the old weariness came back again when I
breathed the air of the school-room once more."

"But go where the air is full of ozone—go to the
seashore!"

"Haven't I been to the seashore! Surely you don't
forget our Boothbay enjoyments, and don't you remember Magnolia and its delights?"

"Oh, yes, Jean, but there is one place you have not
visited—one page you have not turned. They say it is
unique and fascinating in its very strangeness. They
say there is fresh air and pure water, good food and the
best society; besides amber sunsets and glorious moon-
rises over the ocean, and surf-bathing, and shell-gather-
ing and—for you who love botany so well—plenty of
wild flowers, and simplicity of living, and quaint houses
and honest people, and——

"And,—and,—and—why, my dear, who told you all
this, and where is the wonderful place?"

"Don't laugh, Jean, I've been reading ''Sconset Cottage Life,' by a wide-awake Syracuse lawyer, who loves
the woods and the fields and the sea, as well as you do,
and his book has a wonderful charm for weary people,
I've heard say. At any rate, it has charmed me, and I
want you to say you'll go to Nantucket Island and rest
awhile. I'll do all the packing, attend to all the details,

and you shall have no care and no trouble. Only say you'll go, for I am sure it will do you a world of good."

"Well, Helen," said the invalid—for she was something of an invalid, albeit she ignored the title, and had not failed to perform faithfully her duties in the school-room; but the languid step and the heavy eye told of the wear and tear of the nerves that, after sleepless nights of pain, had been rasped and worn by the countless and unavoidable jars of the school-room. She loved her work as a teacher, she was beloved by the children in her charge, she was a trusted friend of their parents, and a favorite with the school-board; but the more than a quarter of a century of steady, faithful effort had done its work upon the physical powers that were not deathless, and there was need of rest and recuperation, or the school-room would have to be forsaken, and to the noble work of the teacher she must say "good-bye" forever. There had been intervals in her school-work— interregnums that were filled with work in the hospitals, when our wounded soldier boys watched her coming as that of an angel, when she wrote for them, read to them, sang for them, prayed with them,—and sometimes closed their eyes for the last, long slumber, and then wrote the sad letter to the home friends, which told them of an accepted sacrifice and a returnless path. She never for-

got to speak of the mansions in the Father's house, and
the dear Christ who had welcomed their noble boys to
the home He had gone to prepare.   And so her name was
embalmed in many hearts.   She had given one year also
to the schools of the South, and in that city where the
Libby prison had been the awful doom of many a brave
soldier boy—she taught, in the first year of peace, the
earliest public school for white children.·   And the
children of rebellious men became her loyal supporters,
for "the law of kindness dwelt upon her lips," and
while abhorring treason, she never ceased to love and
care for the traitor's little ones as faithfully as she cared
for those whose fathers enlisted under the flag her own
loyal brothers were enlisted under, and for whose safety
and honor one of those dear brothers died.   So, far and
near, this Massachusetts teacher had a host of friends,
but none of them could stay the progress of disease,
possibly, as some thought, induced, amid the self-deny-
ing labors of the hospital, fostered by a continuance of
residence in an enervating climate with wearying school
labors, and fastened by a month in the Log Cabin on
Centennial Grounds, where she helped to make memorable and enjoyable the visits of thousands to that struc-
ture, whose appearance and furniture was a historic
delight, charming the antiquarian, and instructing the

foreigner who had just begun to learn of the Mayflower
and her pilgrims, of Miles Standish and his victories, of
Concord, Lexington and Bunker Hill. Now she was
worn and weak and weary. Pain had become a con-
tinual presence, and sleeplessness intensified pain. So
the energetic, warm-hearted Helen longed to try some
new remedy, and delightedly urged a trial of 'Sconset
cottage life, and waited only till the words, " Well,
Helen," were succeeded by a look which signified " the
question is settled; do as you think best."

It did not take Helen long to pack that trunk. Sister
Beth, whom they visited before leaving—the good farmer's wife, and the farmer's good wife—soon had lunch
ready, the ruddy, whole-souled nephews of the farm
harnessed the strong horses, the handsome nieces kissed
the departing aunts, Tip barked, Gyp struggled to get
out of detaining arms to follow her mistress, but was
reluctantly left, and soon they were on their way to
Boston. In the Old Colony Depot a sweet-faced lady
waited to bid them " Good-bye," and placed parting
gifts of books and fruits in the dear invalid's hands.
Other loved friends were there to say " farewell"—some
of "Christ's little lambs" were there also, one tearfully
wishing she could go to Nantucket with them, and
cheered with the promise that she should follow them

soon; and one was there who claimed the far-famed
island as her birthplace, and was about to make her annual visit to the Mecca of her heart.   The hour came—
the cry of " All aboard " was heard and they moved out
of the depot and toward the rest and peace and refreshment of ocean breezes and sunny skies and pleasant
homes and warm and happy hearts.

A few hours of comfortable car-riding—not over
warm, nor very dusty; through stretches of farming country—through pine groves—through busy little towns,
and catching delightful glimpses toward the end of the
journey of blue waters and sandy beaches, of rocking
boats and snowy sails—and then they landed upon the
wharf, waited a short season in the depot, secured a nice
cup of coffee, and conversed with the pleasant faced
young woman who manipulated the telegraphic keys
with great success, and then a cry rose—"There she is,
there comes the 'River Queen'!"   The uninitiated
looked in various directions.   The older travellers saw
the smoke-stack moving apparently over the land not
far away, and in a few moments the people from New
Bedford were landing at Wood's Holl, the passengers
for Oak Bluffs and Nantucket thronged the plank in
their stead, the trunks were hastily wheeled on board,
with the usual amount of shouting and screaming, of
warning and command.

At last, the plank was drawn in, but in a half hour,
more or less, it was out again; the larger number of passengers scattered themselves in the hotels and cottages
of Oak Bluffs, and then the seekers after real rest and
solid comfort steamed away for the historic island.

CHAPTER II.

LAND HO !

"Oh, know ye that Isle ?   'Tis the isle of my fathers,
  The island that gave my first breathings to me ;
  And still, through long absence, far memory gathers
  Its brightest and best from that Isle of the Sea."

HENRY GLOVER.

ON and on we steamed.   The blue waters rolled beneath us.   The white sea-gulls screamed, and soared, and wheeled, and dipped around us.   Here was a buoy to mark a shoal, there a black, low, freight-laden propeller, yonder a yacht with snowy sails, farther off a topsail schooner; low on the horizon a brig with all sails set, and close aboard, soon, a fishing smack.   Then we descried a light-boat riding the waves with her lantern hung amidships on the mast, while the faithful crew were some of them sleeping, in needful preparation for their vigilant night watches.   The exhilarating sea-breeze dropped to a calm—a light fog arose—it grew more dense—the eager eyes that scanned the horizon

for the first outline of the beloved island were disap-
pointed. Not this time were they to see that, which
to them was more beautiful than Venus, rising out of
the sea. But the fog lifted, or the steamboat pushed
steadily through and out of its enveloping folds, and
there was the old island; far off to the left the white
tower of the light-house at Great Point ; on the right the
little island of Tuckernuck, named by the Indians, from
its shape, that of a loaf of bread. In front, the water-
tank on its stilts—the Cliff, with its ancient houses and
modern cottages, the Jetty, stretching its stony length
towards the channel—the bell buoy—Brant Point light
—and soon the town of Nantucket rising in its amphi-
theatrical dignity—so often mentioned by travellers—
full before our eyes.

We drew nearer and more near. There was the
crowd upon the wharf. There were the carriages, public and private—but the place where the boat would land
its passengers was well enclosed. No pushing and crowd-
ing near the plank, but such a volley from the farther
off eyes of hundreds! We stand upon the upper deck.
A hand is waving! There waves a handkerchief! We
cannot tell, as we slowly take our place at the wharf,
whose hand it is, or whether the token is for us or for
another. But "there's George!" shouts one of our

2

party. "There's the wagon!" screams another, "yes,
and Rollie!"   And they all go below, and go ashore,
and such a getting into all sorts of vehicles, and so many
pleasant greetings, and such warnings to "wrap up, if
you are going to 'Sconset to-night, for its growing thick
again!"   "Only a sea-fog!" says the quiet brother,
with a suggestion as to how heavy-weights should be
stowed in such a wagon as he had brought—large,
roomy, easy, and with secured seats, but with no cover-
ing ; therefore the umbrellas were placed so as to be
handy.   The crowd had been disintegrating while our
party was finding baggage and hoisting themselves—
Helen right over the wheel—into the commodious vehi-
cle, and the wagon, as it rattled off the wharf and over
the cobble stones, passed pedestrians of every size, while
the occupants noticed that door-steps and windows were
thronged with people who gazed on the new-comers
ready to return the salute of friendship or the greeting
of good-will.   Along Federal Street, where "the Atheneum" was pointed out with commendable pride by the
natives to the visitors in the wagon, and across and up
Main Street to Orange, where the town clock in the
venerable church is mentioned as the generous gift of a
successful son of Nantucket, who also gilded the dome
of his childhood's Sabbath home, down Orange Street,

past "the Block" where the earnest woman pastor re-
sides, past the "Sherburne House" and the "Bay View,"
and other hotels and boarding houses which are seen and
mentioned, with scraps of their early history thrown in,
and the owners of the long ago remembered with a sigh
or smile—with a loving hand-shake from kindred who
rush from their door for a moment to the wagon—on to
"Newtown gate," (no gate at all), crossing the railroad
track (!!) looking at the comfortable Almshouse, peering
along the road to see if other carriages are bound 'Scon-
setward, and then the night and the fog settles down,
waterproofs and umbrellas come into use, and the horse
jogs along in the rut; conversation flags, and the wish
comes that the cars, instead of going only to the South
Shore as they did then, could land the weary passengers
from the boat, in a short hour at 'Sconset.   By-and-by
they came to a sort of parting of the roads—at least to
a sandy space from whence many rutted roads proceed.
"Which will you take, George?" is the inquiry.   "Oh!"
said the driver, who was farmer, ex-mariner, fisherman
and brother all in one, besides being a husband and the
father of six likely children—"It doesn't matter, for
whichever road you choose you'll wish you had taken the
other," and they jogged on.   The sandy road and the
heavy cargo were not promotive of great speed, so the fog

had ample opportunity to sift itself in and around the
invalid, and awakened the ever-vigilant Helen to a fear
that the rheumatism might be augmented, or the misty-
moisty voyage in the wagon across the curtained plains,
result in pulmonary dangers.   " No fear of the fog!"
persisted the cheery driver, bound to look on the bright
side. " People never get cold in a sea-fog!"   But the
fog changed to a drizzling rain—at least a trifle worse
than a Scotch mist.   Then it lifted a little.   Far off
was seen the flash of Sancoty, and then arose a conversation upon the merits of that wonderful Fresnel Light,
which could be seen, in clear nights, for twenty miles at
sea, and warned off many a mariner from the dangerous
South Shoals.

  All at once a smell—an odor—a fragrance! Quick
senses discern quickly, and one at least of the travellers
was on the alert.   "Swamp flowers! I guess"—said one,
" Swamp pinks!" said the driver, " Swamp azaleas!" exclaimed Helen, with an irrepressible " Oh, I must have
some! I must have some !"   The good natured driver
said " Whoa !" kindly dismounted, then following the
scent, he gathered from the swampy roadside the fragrant blossoms of the " clethra " and a few scattered
specimens of the wild azalea.

  " There's health in the very aroma of the wild flowers

here!" said Helen, and she eagerly placed them in her sister's hands, and then she told her how from early spring to the coming of snow-flakes there are flowers along those Nantucket swamps and all over the plains. The trailing arbutus sends abroad its delicious fragrance with the coming of the blue birds, and the golden-rod and aster display their beauty in the shortened sunbeams of the dying year. The moisture of the atmosphere, as in the British Isles, is conducive to the brilliant coloring of the flowers, and yellower buttercups or more golden dandelions are nowhere to be found. The little *housatonia* whitens the roadsides at one time, and later the *Hudsonia* gilds the plains, then the purple *geradia*, the yellow aster, the pink *polygala*, the Indian bean, the sickle-leaved *inula*—each in its own season—appear. On the margin of some of the little ponds grows the lovely, starry, pink *sabbatia;* and Nantucket botanists pride themselves on saying that the veritable *erica cineria* (with other heather plants) the real Scotch heather, is to be found in a few secluded and unnamed spots, which, on the authority of Prof. Gray, they declare grows in no other place throughout the length and breadth of these United States—perhaps, I should say, not in all America.

Conversing of these flowers (the natives, it must be

confessed, boasting a little) the travellers proceeded.
The village was reached at last.   Its windows could be
seen, for the cheerful light shone from within.

" There swings Robert's lantern! " exclaimed one.

" And there's Aunt Sophy's big lantern! " said another.

But the lanterns were all forgotten—for there was
the new Chapel, just built, picturesque for that inartis-
tic village—all lighted up, the colored lights of its window in front, filling the whole street and village with a
sense of the æsthetic, and packed from the platform to
the doorsteps with 'Sconset folks—natives and visitors—
to listen to the pathos and humor of the sweet-faced
elocutionist, (rejoicing in the Coffin name and blood)
and to be uplifted by the vocal and instrumental music
of that welcomed hour.   'Sconset at last had an audience room large enough for the many, if not for all.
And the little chapel which was hardly finished, and
not yet furnished and dedicated, was utilized at once to
earn its musical instrument, and give the exalted satisfaction of an intellectual and artistic treat to those who
had not forgotten the opera or the theatre, though daily
listening to the voice and music of that mighty ocean,

> " Which rolls the wild, profound eternal bass
> In Nature's anthem, and makes music
> Which can please the ear of God."

The wagon passed on, and soon it stopped before a
little, weather-worn cottage, full of sweet and sacred
memories to many hearts, and there a welcome and sup-
per had been waiting long. They gladly accepted both;
then one of them found her way to the chapel for the
sake of the dear faces to be seen as well as for the enter-
tainment. The latter was almost over, but the full
quarter's worth of joy and more was had in the friendly
greetings, and the great satisfaction, that at last the long
desired goal was reached, and one of the things dear to
the heart of Siasconset was attained.

Long after the chapel lights were out, and the audience scattered, the little cottage was full of activity.
The invalid chose to occupy "the sky parlor," and
found the few stairs of the lowly dwelling not very hard
to climb. Carefully walking somewhat near the center
of the two bedrooms nearest the ridge-pole, heads were
safe from contact with the beams, darkened with age,
but swept neatly from cobwebs and their occupants.
The air, though moist, was not unrefreshing, nor dis-
agreeable. No musquitoes sang a requiem at the death
of comfort, nor danced their provoking war-dances in
our very faces.

The weary ones laid their heads upon their pillows.
There was a murmur of prayer, and that was succeeded

by the murmuring of the waves, heard in the stillness of the night, and never ceasing, rising and falling, as the breakers gathered and broke, and gathered yet again. All night long the light-house fire blazed, and flashed and blazed again, and all night long, while the fog lifted and the stars came out, and the soft breeze stirred the white curtains in the little cottage, and the sleepers rested, sounded far and near the solemn roaring of the mighty sea.

CHAPTER III.

SURROUNDINGS IN THE COTTAGE.

" But the stranger there finds, in each humble dwelling,
  Kind brotherly greeting, hearts open and free;
  And prayers for the humble far upwards are swelling
  From each lonely shrine in that Isle of the Sea."

HENRY GLOVER.

MORNING came with the glory of sunshine, and the inmates of the little cottage were early astir. Vacation hours seemed too precious to be spent in sleep, though very often, sleep is the best medicine for the weary body and the overtasked mind.

"What will you do first?" exclaimed Jean, after breakfast was over, and the determined look on the otherwise pleasant countenance of the active Helen, was supplemented by the emphatic answer—"Do! the trunks are to be emptied, in part, at least, and we are to get settled."

"Getting settled" meant much locomotion, many words, and not a few audible smiles.

"Do give me the attic chamber, Helen," was the ap-
peal of the invalid sister. "It is airy, by reason of the
good draught, if it is not so very lofty, and its very
quaintness, and being so much the opposite of what I
have at home, is attractive to me."

"Oh! yes, Jean, you shall have your way. Under the
roof here at 'Sconset, does not mean the excessive heat
and discomfort of a garret in other places. Pure air
and plenty of it—heat tempered by the proximity of
the ocean—that's what 'Sconset means! Besides, if you
want to bathe in the ocean water, while you are yet too
lame to go into the surf, you can be retired enough and
yet warm enough to have your fresh pail of water every
day brought to you, and bathe in your chamber."

"*Fresh* pail of *salt* water, Helen! How that sounds!
But never mind, if I only get the water with sufficient
saline and other qualities to make me well again. This
state of invalidism is foreign to my taste, as well as custom, and I long for the buoyant health I have enjoyed
most of my life."

"Well, Nantucket is said to be a place of recuperation. If health can be regained anywhere, it can here.
The old residents, you see, are healthy enough, and they
live to great age here, with a vigor of mind and body
that makes life desirable."

"Yes, but who knows whether it is the hygienic qualities of the ozone atmosphere, and the purity of the
water, and the restful character of the social life, which
moves with an unruffled flow, or whether it is the in-
herited longevity of men and women whose ancestors
were possessed of more than common physical stamina,
and lived very clean and therefore healthy lives."

"What's the use of reasoning over the matter"! spoke
up the Native Member of the party, "just do the best
you can.   Here's Father Coffin, hale and hearty for a
man almost four score ; and Captain Baxter, whom
you'll see pretty soon, a younger man at eighty than
some men of forty—and his wife's uncle, that you will
see moving about the bank, in the dignity of venerable
age and a worthy record, almost ninety, yet able to converse as intelligently as ever, his memory scarcely failing,
and his remarkable powers of mind so evident that one
has no reason to wonder why his daughters are such
superior teachers.   I tell you, Capt. Swain is a specimen
for a Nantucketer to be proud of, and all you have to
do, is to enjoy seeing such encouraging instances of
health and long life, and make up your mind that
'Sconset will build you up again, and give you another
lease of life and health."

So they talked on till "Jean! Jean!" was the cry of

the stirring member, Helen, who had rushed away while
the N. M. was talking, "you'd better stop arguing the
question, and come up here, and see what I've done,
while you've been talking. 'Save your breath to cool
your porridge.' Come up here!"

They ascended. This 'Sconset cottage rejoiced in a
flight of real stairs, and at the top was a door opening
into a comfortable chamber, with sloping roofs, but
lathed and ready for plastering. The laths however
were nailed there long years before—and more than two
decades of 'Sconset air and wear had browned them almost to the color of mahogany. In the room was a
bedstead with one of the most comfortable of beds upon
it, and Helen had it invitingly prepared already for the
second night. An ancient, oaken desk, with sloping
top, stood in a niche under the roof, and nearer the
door stood a mahogany bureau, both of these historic in
that household, and therefore highly prized, though
bearing the evidence of much use and great age. Over
the bureau was a mirror, with carved, mahogany frame.
From one lower corner a piece of the glass had been
broken, but Helen had covered up the vacant space,
and gratified her æsthetic proclivities by placing a bunch
of artificial roses in the corner.

Across a little passage way, which led to the attic

over the back part of the cottage, they stepped, doors
opened from each chamber into the passage, which
could be closed for privacy or opened for the fresh, cool
breeze from the wide ocean, glimpses of which could be
seen from the two eastern windows.   This western
chamber was the special retreat of the invalid, for repose and refreshment.   Two bedsteads were here—one
of them the well-known cot bedstead with sacking bottom, so common in many homes on the island for use on
extra occasions, because easily borne from place to place.
The nurse occupied it nights, and the infant day-times,
on those memorable occasions when the mother had
gone down to the gates of the grave after the children
who were to make glad the hearth and home in coming
years;—and not infrequently it was the last resting
place of the beloved but forsaken forms which awaited
the final transfer to the burial casket, in the sacred and
solemn repose of a nobly finished work and a peacefully
ended life.   White curtains, small and plain, were at
the windows.   Helen had found two old cloaks, of cam-
let and bombazine, and stretched them along the wall
" for tapestry "—as she said;—a small, old table which
she had discovered out in the yard with the grass growing up and around its worm-eaten legs, was utilized—
covered by a snowy towel with a scarlet, embroidered

end—back of it against the dark beams and laths, was
the top of a cherry table—inlaid—and on it a glass
tumbler of sweet and showy flowers. There was the
clethra for fragrance, the red field lily for color, the
sunflower for æsthetic significance. And sunflowers
were to be had for the gathering—since in the little
vegetable garden near the cottage, the boy-farmers who
called these 'Sconset visitors "Aunties," had planted
sunflowers enough to gladden, with their black and
shiny seeds, the winter days of the flock of hens the busy
boys were cherishing as chickens through the Summer
hours. In their golden glory the sunflowers towered and
nodded, and were of all sizes and various stages of advancement, bloom and ripeness.

" *Helianthus annuus !*" exclaimed Jean, "I welcome
you to my boudoir!"

"Oscar would be delighted to see your flowers, Jean,"
laughed Helen.

"But," said the N. M. thoughtfully, for somehow
the jokes always grew to be matter-of-fact with her,
"the sunflower ought to be cultivated more than it is.
Valuable to the farmer by its seeds which the fowl so
greedily appropriate, it is yet more valuable as a rapid
grower in malarial districts. Its leaves are like the
Scripture ones—'for the healing of the nations.' All

our cities need improvement societies to insist upon sunflowers in every back-yard, lane and alley."

"Do make yourself a committee of one," said Helen, "to spread abroad the virtues of the sunflower. Perhaps Oscar Wilde would like a partnership engagement. You do the practical part and he the posturing and æsthetic."

"Farewell to Oscar!" was the reply of the Native Member, "and farewell to both of you. I'm going down to take my things out of my trunk, and make the little front parlor into a study. When you are ready, Jean, my nephew will call in to talk with you about German lessons, and while you are teaching him to say ' *Guten Morgen !*' I'll begin on your copy of Carlyle."

She tripped away, but Helen called after her, "Don't be poking over a book all the time, while you are at 'Sconset. You read enough at home. Take out your photographs of the children and grandchildren, and other celebrities, if there are any equal to those grandchildren, and put them up around the table and on the mantel. Make yourself useful, for once."

The N. M. laughed, and declaring there was freedom at 'Sconset, nevertheless obeyed. Soon the trio were at work, and lo! a transformation scene, equal to the one just enacted overhead. Sunlight invaded the premises, always scrupulously clean, but always kept free from dust

by the closing of all apertures, and with the lowered
muslin and outside paper curtains kept generally darkened.   Away up to the top went the outside curtains,
half way up the white ones, then the window was opened,
the table placed in front, (its green cloth covered with
a white towel) for ink, and pens, and paper, and postal
cards, and all the paraphernalia of a study-table; rows
of books were placed there also; in the corner a rocking-
chair for Jean ; a corner sacred to the invalid henceforth
—and the work was done.   On the mantel in front of
the plain, old-time looking-glass, stood the framed pictures of the little ones, the great-grandchildren of the
owner of the cottage, and on the walls were tacked in-
numerable photographs of distant friends, more or less
distinguished in the world of letters or in society.

    " Why the little room is a gem!" exclaimed Jean, who
evinced such a genuine satisfaction in all the efforts made
for her comfort, that it was a pleasure to devise and
execute plans with that end in view.

    Forthwith she seated herself in her cosy corner, and
her pen began to travel back and forth over one of
those handy pieces of card-board the Government has
wisely devised for saving time and fostering the expression of good will.   And oh! the postals and letters that
went forth from that cottage! Native and foreign mem-

bers of that household vied with each other in sending
back to the Continent of America, and far away to
Europe also, missives of remembrance and affection,
never failing to declare that 'Sconset was a grand place
for recuperation and rest, with neither fuss nor feathers,
starch nor sentiment, to make life unbearable, and that
they wished all their correspondents could breathe that
air and drink that water, and share the freedom from
conventionality, in the atmosphere of good-will, which
was best and most healthful of all.

The neighbors had been in, a few of them, more came
later in the week, but all expressed a desire that the
weary ones should be refreshed, that the invalid should
recover health, that the N. M. should enjoy her island
birth-place—albeit eight miles away from the little
street, now a garden, and the old-fashioned house,
burned in the great fire of 1846, where she first saw the
light.   Godfrey erroneously calls her a native of
'Sconset, but, perhaps it matters little, for from the
sands of Smith's Point to those of Great Point, from the
Cliff to Sancoty and 'Sconset Bank, including the
picturesque town upon her several hills, all is Nantucket
Island, and the N. M. is proud to be known as a Nantucketer.

And pleasant were the seasons of literary communion

and converse in that little front room. There the trio
used to sit with their books and pens when the house-
work was finished. The student-nephew would run in
with some flower or shell about which he would have
some question to ask or some fact to state. Voices
could be heard from the bench in front of the little
store, as the owner and his neighbors sat there on the
bench under the awning, chatting of the lively work the
carpenters were making along the bank, or telling old-
time stories of whaling victories and fishermen's dangers.
The pretentious "Grocery" on the Main Street had
taken most of the custom from this little store, and left
the gray-haired sea-captain plenty of leisure to fight his
ocean battles over again with the new-comers who sometimes questioned saucily, to find that the seeming simplicity of the aged mariner was a match for their inquisi-
tiveness. Sometimes a savory smell from the kitchen
would creep in unasked and give evidence that Helen's
activity was finding new outlet, evidence that was em-
phasized when, descrying old friends just returned from
Europe, riding up to the house, she rushed to the door,
and warmly welcomed them, crying aloud, "Come in!
come in! I've got some jolly good gingerbread for you!"
Didn't that white-haired, handsome gentleman and his
elegant lady-wife prize that hearty home welcome!

And the Egyptologist and his literary life companion ate the gingerbread—"and gave thanks."

So, in the little bed-rooms, trim and neat, with old-fashioned but comfortable furniture; in the large sitting-room, where the family gathered as it grew larger; in the great, convenient kitchen, with its sink and pantry and pot-closets, its old desk and sizable stove, its rag-carpet and ancient chairs—as well as in the airy chambers and cosy study the 'Sconset visitors found comfort and rest.

Pleasant greetings from the dwellers in the village met them on every hand, and often a neighborly call was made by a cheery spirit which of itself served to energize the invalid and help her to feel that life was yet worth living.

How handsome she looked, with her regular features, specially fine eyes, and dark, wavy hair, sitting in the rocking-chair in her corner, wrapped in her scarlet robe, and ready with a kind word, or a sprightly repartee, or calling upon the others to pause while she read from her favorite Emerson and Carlyle! And well she realized the truth of what the former said in his essay on "Power."

"The first wealth is health. Sickness is poor-spirited, and cannot serve anyone; it must husband its resources

to live.   But health or fullness answers its own ends,
and has to spare, runs over, and inundates the neighbor-
hoods and creeks of other men's necessities."

So she rejoiced in her surroundings as conducive to
health, but most of all she rejoiced in the evidence that
sympathy was an island commodity, and that invalidism
touches not only the sands and surf but the homes, not
only the hands but the hearts, of Siasconset.

CHAPTER IV.

SURF—BATHING.

" Again to thee, O surf-encircled strand,
   Enamored still my thoughts will turn ; once more,
   Dear Siasconset, by thy foam-clad shore,
  Leaving in thought this tree-encumbered land,
  How well I love to tread thy arid sand,
   And listen to thy waves' sonorous roar !' "

CHARLES F. BRIGGS.

NOW, sister Jean, you are going to the beach! What is the use of being so near the surf, and never seeing the bathers! Suppose you are not able to go in yourself, it will do you good to see other folks tumble about in the water."

Jean thought so too, and therefore Helen made all needful preparations. A shawl to spread on the sands, where the invalid might sit ; another to throw over her shoulders if the sea-breeze proved too cool, a basket for shells, if any were found, and a parasol to shield her from the sun's rays if more shade was needed than her large-brimmed, shore hat would afford.

"Don't forget the opera-glass!" exclaimed the N. M.,
"I've been used to a spy-glass all my life—at least all
my earlier days—and you'll find I'm right in saying this
glass will help you to see the wonderful and the beautiful around you on the beach."

"And what's that under your left arm?" asked
Helen. "I declare, it's a book! I might have known
it was. I could have guessed with my eyes shut. Of
course, you would'nt be happy on that glorious beach
without a book! I verily believe you'd want one if you
were walking the golden streets, and you wouldn't be
happy with the angels if they don't have libraries."

"Now, Helen!" remonstrated the N. M., "what do
you care for! Why not let everybody be happy each in
his own way!"

"Because, you precious simpleton—don't you know
you need a change? Do let your eyes and your mind
rest, for one week, at least!"

"La! never mind what Helen says!" cried the peace-
making Jean," you know she wants us all to be benefited
by our 'Sconset sojourn. And for this once let's leave
the book."

"O, I am no 'slave to the lamp,'" answered the N. M.,
"I can study and learn without a book, except Nature's
Illuminated Volume, and Helen knows that is wide open.

at 'Sconset. Come Helen, you dear careful-and-troubled-
about-many-things-Helen! and don't forget your ' tent
on the beach!' "

" ' Tent on the Beach!' Whittier's? Why I thought
she would not have us take a book. What does she
mean by taking one herself?" asked Jean.

But the N. M. did not need to answer, for Helen, with
characteristic gesture and the air of a *tragedienne*, whom
she much resembled, shouted—" ' Infirm of purpose,
give me the ' tent!" and forthwith spread a large, light-
colored umbrella with a green lining, and marched off
in the direction of the beach. Very good service did
that "tent" do, on the beach, and elsewhere during that
summer sojourn by the sea. And its size and color
helped one who was seeking its owner easily to find her,
when the bathing spot was thronged with its hundreds
of happy mermaids and their attendants.

Only a little distance, through the short, narrow,
grass-lined paths, now dignified with the name of
streets, henceforth—from 1883 on—to be immortalized
in the diaries of those whose cottages are on them, and
as the headings to their letters, whisked away by scores
in Capt. Baxter's wagon every day. When only the villagers were at 'Sconset there was no need of anything
to mark the places of residence, for everybody knew

where every other body lived, and it was enough to say,
"Gone to Capt. Pitman's, or Uncle Alfred's, or William
Owen's, or to *the* pump, or his boat-house," and at once
the inquirer would know how to proceed to find the man
he sought.   But when "the strangers"—so-called—began to come, they lived one season in one cottage, and
the next season in another, so finally, they named their
cottages various fanciful names, and the original owners
were lost sight of, in the fashionable nomenclature of
the thronging visitors.   Then the streets were named,
and one day, when the N. M. and her friends were returning from the beach, they found white signboards
with black lettering, informing them that henceforth the
hotels were on Main Street.   They had crossed Broad-
way, and their own domicile was on New Street, which,
as it had been laid out forty years before, was rather a
misnomer.   But the new grows old always and everywhere.   Thank God the old grows new again.

> "But still the new transcends the old,
>   In signs and tokens manifold :"

and the thoughtful and trustful will not murmur,

> "For all of good the Past has had
>   Remains to make our own time glad,
>   Our common, daily life divine,
>   And every land a Palestine."

It was, therefore, no marvel that the trio, who went forth from the "Coffyn Cottage" on New Street, stood for a season, in rapt admiration, on the bank at the head of the curving path which sloped down to the sandy beach. The green grass lined that path, and the thistles in their purple splendor, with the showy stramonium, blossomed on the side toward the hill. But, before their feet could press the pebbly road, the wide ocean called for their attention, and every eye was bent upon the waves that flashed beneath the sunshine, then rolled and curved and broke in long, white lines upon the sandy shore.

It was the bathing hour. Soon the clocks in the little cottages would strike eleven. "Straggling down the bank," to use Mr. Northrop's graphic, if not elegant, phrase," came the bathers, men, women and children— in motley suits passing all description, fantastic and uncouth, neat and artistic, faded and forlorn, bright and gay, span new and clean, and mottled with clinging kelp—costumes baggy, short in the extremities, disguising beauty, and giving ugliness a new horror, dresses bewitching in the revelation of white arms and fair necks,—all sorts, indeed, and amazingly amusing to a fresh comer to 'Sconset. Down they came to the two or three chosen bathing grounds, where a stout rope

The Curving Path—page 41.

stretched over a support on shore extended out forty or
fifty feet to a barrel which sustained it and beyond
which it was finally anchored,—a contrivance which
gave confidence and courage to the most timid." All
this, so well described in "'Sconset Cottage Life"—the
trio from "Coffyn Cottage" saw, and enjoyed. The
novelty of it all, the breezy hill-top,—the winding, sloping path, stony and somewhat steep, to the sandy beach—
the wide stretch of yielding sands over which a plank
pathway led to the border of the surf-wet portion, the
hammocks there swung under awnings, the busy, cheerful crowd, laughing at the mishaps of those who did
not wish a wetting, and yet ventured too near the
sweeping waters of the breaker which had combed and
curved and broke upon the shore—the novelty of it all,
and the exhilaration of it all—was magical to the invalid; and she had not long gazed upon the scene from
the top of the bank, when she announced her intention
of seeking the water-side, and but a short time elapsed
before she was sitting on the out-spread shawl, half re-
clining, with her hands in the warm, clean beach-sand,
exclaiming as it ran through her lifted fingers, "This is
tonic indeed! This is surely Hygiea's kingdom!"

Not far from the party sat a man who watched the
bathers, ready at a moment to spring for a strangling

bather, upset in the frolicsome surf. Sturdy and sober
and solemn, but his sharp eyes in every place at once, it
seemed, and full of interest in new comers or old settlers, alike, if they were in the water, he seemed the
guardian angel of the place. A roughly dressed angel,
to be sure, without wings or sheen, but with a sailor's
heart full of good-will towards the helpless, which
would lead him to rescue the darling of some earthly
home, (if the wild waters swept such a one away from
the rope,) and thereby cause joy in the presence of the
angels of home.

"Here comes Walter!" exclaimed a young girl near
the invalid. Jean turned her head in the direction indicated, and saw a form clad in a bathing suit of blue,
scant but sufficient, advancing toward the surf like a
wheel. And into the water he wheeled—under the
waves—out of sight, then rising he rode calmly on the
surface, beyond the surf, as if the entering upon Nep-
tune's domains in such a way had been the merest
pastime, and was the customary and orderly method.
"Look at Em.!" was the next exclamation, and lo! a
girl, clad in bathing costume all hairy with sea-weed,
advanced like a queen of the mermaids. One glance at
her brother—one scream in a joyous tone, "Coming,
Walter!" and as the great wave rose and began to bow

gracefully towards the spectators, Emily went through
its green-glazed curtains, out of sight, the wave bowed
low upon the sand with a roar of satisfaction, and the
brave girl was at once seen, as the waters rolled up and
then back, far out beyond the line of surf, floating, by
turns, and swimming, beside her only brother. She
had earned much commendation by just such acts of
physical bravery and skill. There were not wanting
those upon the beach who remembered a day when her
body, limp and water-soaked, and with little evidence
that it still held the immortal spark, was rescued, and
borne to her home upon the bank. But as they told
that story they told also the indomitable courage, and
inflexible will which braved all the dangers again and
again till the rightly formed purpose to be a swimmer
was entirely fulfilled. The name she bore indicated that
she might be of the "knowing Folgers," but the strong
will of old Tristram Coffin had come down through her
mother's ancestry, and no one could call her "lazy." As
she swept the mighty waves with her small, but strong
arms, the little lady seemed a very Undine—a goddess of
the deep. She divided the honors of that queenly place,
with others of the island blood, and noticeably with the
handsome elocutionist who had charmed the hearers in
the little chapel. Many a fair lady from other States

than the good old commonwealth the Pilgrims started,
vied with the heroines of 'Sconset heritage and Nantucket name in displaying marvellous skill as swimmers,
and won the rapturous or wondering applause of the
on-looking crowd upon the beach. Beyond the breakers
where the keg that marked the anchorage of the rope,
bobbed and surged and curvetted, there was a motley
gathering of men and boys ; some climbed upon the
keg, some held the rope, and rested, half-floating on
the heaving surges ; and farther north than the rope
and its crowd, was seen one woman with a huge hat
shading her face, and a tall, stalwart youth holding her
by the hands, as she rose and fell amid the breakers that
curled and swept around her.   It was the wife of a well-
known physician who had found large measure of health
in visiting 'Sconset, and whose family, for many long
years, made an annual and often prolonged visit to
the village by the sea, till they came to be regarded
as almost a necessary part of the village itself.   Boy and
"hobbledehoy" and man, one came till he laid aside the
"Master" for "Mr." and supplemented that at last with
"Dr.," having kept the favor of his boyhood's friends,
through all the years of growth and consequent change.

At one point on the beach, not far from the bathers,
a tall, young man was teaching his lady pupils to swim.

The fair-haired youth was a student, reaching out after useful and honorable manhood as a physician, and during his vacation weeks, earning in this way the means to continue his studies. A favorite with all, from his gentle ways, he had the good-will of the host who seek for rest upon the sea shore, because life at all other times is a struggle and an aspiration, which here seems realization and repose. Ambitious youth, clad in the mail of rectitude, does not fight the battles of the world without sympathy, both human and divine.

And now the bathers begin to feel that they have stayed their allotted time, whatever that may be, some a longer and some a shorter time, and they rush up across the beach to the fish-houses, or bath-houses, where they have left their dry clothing. Some of them have prepared for the water while in their cottage homes on the bank, in the village, and even at the hotel, and these wrap their wet selves in a water-proof, put rubbers on their wet and sandy feet, and start, at a brisk pace across the plank-road to their homes.

The trio remain, with others, awhile longer. There is coming and going for an hour or more. One o'clock is the hotel dining-hour, and by that time the bathers will have washed off in fresh water, arranged their toilet, and are ready for a hearty meal.

Meanwhile, the trio return to "Coffyn Cottage."
The aged proprietor believes in noon dinners, and they
are, happily, not much behind time. Then they eat
with 'Sconset appetite, and fall at once into the 'Sconset
habit of sleeping after dinner; the sleep of care-free
children, it is so sweet and restful.

With what pleasure they all read over, at the sunset
hour, the inimitable chapter on "Surf Bathing," in
Northrop's charming *bro-chure*. The day had furnished
them fine illustrations, which retentive memories held
for future joy.

CHAPTER V.

SOCIAL LIFE AT 'SCONSET.

" Undecked, unlovely as thou art,
A speck upon the world's great chart,
Thou art our native spot :
And true to nature, still we love,
And by affection still we prove
Thy faults can be forgot."

MARY MITCHELL.

THERE is no escaping one's own atmosphere. And the atmosphere of a true Nantucketer is eminently social. The fact that the early settlers of the island intermarried, and for many generations, could call each other "Cousin" so largely, has had its influence on the social life of the islanders. The hundred years and more of cousining and neighboring has led to a freedom of social communion, and a personal sympathy, and close companionship, which is very delightful to one born and brought up on that sea-girt isle. The tie is a strong one, and when a Nantucketer who has been dwelling year

4

after year among off-islanders returns to his native place, the cordial welcome is an immeasurable joy.

So it was, that when Helen ran in to the sitting-room, and cried; "A message for you, darling!" and the Native Member saw familiar handwriting and read a kind invitation to take dinner in one of the prettiest cottages, she exclaimed, "Oh, how glad I am! It is just like that hospitable Mrs. S——, she knows how much I shall enjoy meeting those old and valued friends."

The invitation included Helen and her sister; and was cordially received by all. That evening, however, the N. M. was on the sick list, and the invalid had a poor spell, so that the ever-active Helen, went from one to the other through the night, and by the time morning came, with its cares, Helen was worn out. And so it came to pass that the invalid and the N. M. having "recruited," went over to the cottage, and the faithful Helen, having sped the parting guests, sought the seclusion of the tapestried chamber and found rest in the "sleep that knits up the ravelled sleeve of care;" taking, also, her pleasure in the knowledge that while she took needful rest, the others were happy and in congenial society. There were two pastors and a pastor's wife, who were not natives, but all the others whom they met were not only of island birth, but of the very best

island blood. And the pastors? why, one of them was
ministering to a Nantucket church, and the other was
his predecessor in the same pulpit. The pastor with a
wife was not a savage in nature, whatever he might be
in name, an air of refinement was the accompaniment of
his handsome features, and those who listened to his
polished discourses, or conversed with him on varied
topics, could not fail to mark the wide and generous
culture which made him worthy of his scholarly fame
among the island students. And his sweet wife was a
worthy helpmeet. The other? He was a stalwart soldier of the cross, both physically and spiritually. He
had exchanged the parish by the sea, for one among the
granite hills, but as often as he returned to the island
which he loved, he found a welcome worthy of the high
place he had won in their hearts while he served so faithfully for years a people critical because cultured, but
genial because the intellect had not been cultivated at
the expense of the affections. That the said pastor re-
ciprocated their interest in him, and shares their devoted attachment to the historic island, was made evident, if not before, at least when the widely known and
ever-welcome "*Inquirer and Mirror*," published these
words from a letter by Rev. J. B. Morrison.

"I love the old island and the mighty sea. It posses-

ses charms to be found nowhere else.   What a people!
What a history!"   And to these words a rythmic response was made through the press one day, by the writer
of these pages, as follows:

" I love the dear island that rests on the wave,
            Whose fossils proclaim it as old as the days
        When the *ostera* dwelt where the blue waters lave
            The far foot of the hill where the beacon fires blaze.

        O Saucoty ! send thy bright flashes afar !
            Let the gleam of thy light cheer the mariner's heart !
        For the isle of Clan-Coffin shines forth like a star
            In the sky of our memories till life shall depart.

        O island beloved, thy sands have a charm,
            Thy flora so fair and thy shells on the strand,
        Thy people at peace, far from city alarm,
            Thy breezes so healthful, while billows so grand

        Roll in from the ocean, so mighty, so vast;
            Where thy sons were as kings in the proud days of yore,
    " Old Island !" I love thee—on thy breast at last
            Let me sink to the rest that shall cease nevermore.

    " What a people " have come from the stalwart and true,
            Old England's fair children who purchased that strand !
    " What a history " they've written, in deeds, as they grew
            To a mighty host scattered in every land !

"Old Island!" God bless thee from Smith's point to Great,
    From the Cliff to Surfside, and from 'Sconset to Town,
May the "mighty sea" bear to thee, early and late,
    Thy children who joy in thy world-wide renown!

O people, whom God, from the first, set apart,
    Proudly humble, before Him in faithfulness toil,
Till your history, graven on Liberty's heart,
    Shall make hallowed ground of our dear native isle!

The hostess at the pretty cottage was a lady of literary
taste and ability, whose ready pen wrote the appropriate
farewell ode which was sung at the celebrated Re-union
of the descendants of Tristram and Dionis Coffyn, in
1881, and as for the others of the party, were they not
all of the same tastes, and sharers in the lofty sentiments and enlarged ideas which mark the *elite* of the
island! It was a characteristic 'Sconset party—differ-
ing but in size from many others often held by the
town's people upon "'Sconset bank."

The N. M. enjoyed the hearty welcome, and the
kindly greetings best of all, for there was in them a flavor
of school days, and childhood's care-free joys which
had been lacking in many a party she had attended
among those perhaps equally brilliant and kindly, but,
alas! "off-islanders." How the N. M. pities those who
cannot talk of the private schools once patronized upon

the island, and to whom the names of John Boadle and
Alice Mitchell and Mary Russell and Sarah C. Easton
are all unknown! The invalid listens and marvels at
the long-continued delight so evident in the recital of
old-time frolics, and juvenile joys. But she learns before she has been at 'Sconset many days what every
visitor perceives, that the memories of childhood on
that island have a perennial charm, and that to those
who trod the town pavements, or crossed the 'Sconset
ruts, in early days, there is no place so dear as that island
—fifteen miles by eight at most—in all the broad earth,
and however far they may roam, the native Nantucketer
always returns with zest to the narrow streets and rutted
roads, and welcomes the roar of the surf at 'Sconset,
and the sonorous music of the old South bell.

The 'Sconset air whetted the appetites, and the excel-
lent food (for the Nantucket cookery is unsurpassed)
soon disappeared when the pleasant party were called to
the noon-tide meal. Then the "sweet converse" continued, a few trips were made to the bank for a look off
over the waters that slept beneath the sun of that summer afternoon, and a listening to the low murmur of the
"little surf," and then the time came when the party
from town must depart. The carriages arrived, the
hostess and her guests all came out of the little cottage,

the key was turned, farewells exchanged, and soon the
party from town were *en route* toward the setting sun,
and the invalid and the N. M. returned to Coffyn Cottage feeling that life had few greater joys than could be
secured in those cottages by the sea, where the social
life was clean and sweet, with lofty thoughts and un-
alloyed good-will.

That was not the only social gathering the N. M. and
her associates enjoyed while inmates of Coffyn Cottage.
Sometimes from town came whole families, bringing, as
is the custom, food already cooked, and then in the cottage the harmless beverages were prepared, and the big
tables placed side by side, and the dishes that were heir-
looms, and some of them sacred with memories of those
who will eat and drink from them no more, placed thereupon; the chairs drawn up; the arm-chair placed for the
aged master of the house, and then the younger and
the older of the company assembled, and hastened to ap-
pease the appetites which 'Sconset only and ever affords,
the viands were soon distributed and disappeared. Fresh
air and sunshine browned the cheeks, but gave a robust
health to the merry youth, and the elder ones shared in
all the outward blessings, and added the cherished
memories and hallowed hopes which always assist in the
preservation of that measure of health which is so much
to be desired, on sea or shore.

There were social evenings at the ancient cottage, when
the neighbors and relatives took an hour or so after dark,
and ran in for a quiet talk.   But the evenings were
short, and after such long and busy days, the invalid
was inclined to seek a bath and repose, while the others,
especially the younger of the relatives, preferred to
ramble over the bank, or down on the beach, or wait
for the mail, out by Capt. Baxter's.   But at last quiet
was secured, no dogs barked, no horse cars rumbled, no
musquito piped a roundelay; silence reigned, unbroken
except by the low murmuring, or solemn roar, of the
surf, while the stars looked down on the peaceful cottages, and there was no fear of burglars or incendiaries,
to hinder the sweet, refreshing sleep so needed by the
invalid, so welcome to the household, one and all.

And the heart of Siasconset—the kindly feeling—
was perceived even in the silent hours, for the heads of
Helen and the N. M. rested on soft pillows which in
this time of full houses and extra needs had been kindly
loaned to the N. M. by one of her girlhood's friends,
and were fragrant as sweet, English clover with the
memories of those far-off days when "thee" and "thy"
were words familiar in both use and hearing, at the
homes of each and in the hours of school.   Surely
Whittier could say—and it would be true—to Linda

and Sarah and to the N. M.—and their hearts would echo the words:—Your hearts, oh! trio of birthright members!—

" How widely soever you've strayed from the fold,
    Though your "thee" has grown "you" and your drab,
        blue and gold,
    To the old friendly speech and the garb's sober form,
    Like the heart of Argyle to the tartan grow warm.

     *   *   *   *   *   *   *

    Who scoffs at our birthright? the words of the seers,
    And the song of the bards in the twilight of years,
    All the foregleams of wisdom in santon and sage,
    In prophet and priest are our true heritage.
    And this green, favored island, so fresh and sea-blown,
    When she counts up the worthies her annals have known,
    Never waits for the pitiful gaugers of sect
    To measure her love, and mete out her respect. "

CHAPTER VI.

A CHAPEL RETROSPECT.

"Thou savedst me from the dangers of the sea,
  That I might bless thy name forevermore,
  Thy love and power the same will ever be
  Thy mercy is an inexhausted store."

                                    PELEG FOLGER.

OOKING out of the window toward the little
chapel one bright morning, the N. M. expressed,
(as she was wont to do, being a little given to repetition
in her expression of thought and emotion, perhaps
owing to her profession, which countenances "line
upon line, and precept upon precept,") her great delight
that the village had at last an edifice in which the
devout heart of Siasconset might voice itself in prayer
and praise.

Then the invalid asked concerning the generosity
which linked the name of Horatio G. Brooks forever
with the land upon which it stood, and the N. M., with
the assistance of Helen—whose memory of details was

unparalleled—recounted the history of the various efforts in the direction of a place of worship; how the
Martins early encouraged the idea, and the village-folk
and towns-people made various contributions to the
sums at first subscribed, till at last, in 1882—the matter
was brought to a pleasant climax by the presentation of
the lot whereon the chapel now stands, and then followed its consecration.

The day previous was a memorable day upon 'Sconset
beach. The surf was very high; the mighty heaving of
the surges appalled the bathers, except that a few of
the more venturesome, thought it would be a good
opportunity to try their powers as swimmers, and a
few others, not realizing the vast force of the surging
waters, imagined they could stand by the rope as usual,
and no harm could come.

One of these latter bathers was a young girl from the
capital of our nation—a teacher in one of the public
schools at Washington. Along the banks of the Poto-
mac there was no such surf, and she was all unused to
the perils of the deep in such an hour. Holding fast
to the rope, she rather enjoyed the fierce buffetings of
the waves, and laughed merrily at the fears of the timid
ones on shore. One gentleman alone was near her, and
he was lame, and as an invalid, could do little for her

rescue, when suddenly a mighty wave swept her from
her hold upon the rope, and tossed her helplessly along
the turbid waters.

Not far from the rope, a clergyman, who believed in
muscular Christianity, had been taking his daily "swim,"
but finding the exertion to be too near the nature of
work to comport with his purpose of play in vacation,
he had reached the shore, and was just going up the
bank to his own cottage, when he heard the loud and
repeated shrieks of those who from the shore and bank
beheld the sad catastrophe, and saw the fair young girl
swept away into the wild swirl of raging waters. His
own wife—nobly forgetting to be selfish—called to him
as a rescuer, and he, taking in at once the danger of the
floating bather, and the necessity of swift assistance,
turned and ran across the beach again to the water-side.
Wildly the surf greeted him with hoarse voice of
triumph, but he plunged in fearlessly—though not a
little weary after his own hard swim, and hard run over
the sands—and struck out 'for the dark object on the
crest of the billow.

The young teacher had retained her presence of mind,
as she was swept away from the rope, so that she placed
herself in position to float, and until she fainted, as the
rescuer reached her side, she had kept her face above
the water.   Then came the struggle.

Anxious eyes watched the brave and difficult feat of the rescuer. Almost exhausted, he yet swam with the maiden till he reached the rope, and there held himself, supporting her, till others came, and both were brought to the shore, the rescuer almost breathless, and so faint and spent that his wife began to fear that in telling him of the great need of his prowess, she had urged him on to his own death. The maiden was beyond all knowledge of events.

Upon a plank she was borne to the nearest cottage on the bank, the doors of which were thrown wide open in Christian hospitality and sympathy. The strong hands of stalwart men bore the imperilled bather to the bed, at once placed at her disposal, and then the heart of Siasconset was still further shown, as the women present began their labor of good-will. Removing the wet clothing, and wrapping her in hot blankets, with bottles of hot water at her feet, and then rubbing vigorously the limbs so chilled, the loving service of the women present was at last rewarded, when the patient opened her dark eyes, and in a weak, plaintive voice, looking earnestly into Helen's eyes (for Helen had rubbed her from the first so vigorously that the perspiration was rolling down her own cheeks) she asked—"Is this death?" "No, this is life," answered Helen, and expressed also her joy that the sufferer could speak. But the revived one looked from face to face. All faces expressed interest, but all were strangers. The answer had not satisfied her. Remembering dimly, as the last thing known, her exceeding peril, and the faint that followed, she seemed to think she had passed through the portal of the grave, and had now come to consciousness upon the other side. Therefore she spoke again.

" Am I dead? Have I died?"

And then one whose face was known to her stepped to her side, and assured her that she was still upon the earth, rescued from the wild waters, and would soon be well as ever again.

And then the request came from the pale sufferer, "Do not let my mother know of this!" for she would not have the news of the peril go to that dear, far off mother, till she could reach her in person and assure her that the peril was no more.

How the heart of Siasconset throbbed in sympathy with the thoughtful devotion of a loving daughter, and in admiration for the noble daring of the muscular under-shepherd who risked his own life to save the imperilled teacher!

This was on Tuesday morning.

The next evening was to see the setting apart of the

donated land to its sacred use, and on Wednesday fore-
noon, Helen and the N. M., with her brother George,
rode over towards Tom Nevers, and there gathered
materials for a wreath, which should be at once sug-
gestive and beautiful as a simple but expressive offering
to the brave rescuer. The heart of Siasconset spoke
its praise and thanks in this, and when the evening
came—but now the press can speak, and the invalid
who had been listening to the story as thus far told, was
then permitted to learn the rest, as Helen read the following account, published in the *Nantucket Inquirer
and Mirror* of Saturday, September 9th, 1882:

"DEDICATION AND THANKSGIVING SERVICE AT
SIASCONSET."

" On Wednesday evening, August 30th, the residents
and summer visitors of Siasconset, young and old, assembled on the plot of ground which has been donated
by Horatio G. Brooks, Esq., of Dunkirk, N. Y., for
the purpose of building thereupon a Union Chapel which
shall be for the use of all denominations, and dedicated
the land thus generously provided for that purpose. At
the same time a service of thanksgiving was held in view
of the rescue from watery graves of Miss Charlotte Garrison (a teacher in Washington, D.C.,) and Rev. Geo. D.

Johnson who went to her assistance and nobly perilled his own life in his successful effort.

"The hour for service was eight and a-half o'clock, and by the light of the moon, just past her full, and two reflectors placed upon the little organ, which had been brought from the school-room, and a lantern held by a friendly hand, the unseated audience united in their first service upon the now consecrated ground.

"Rev. Phebe A. Hanaford announced the hymn— 'Nearer my God to Thee,' which was then sung by all, led by a choir composed of Mrs. Corey, Mrs. Johnson, Mr. Brooks, and others, Mrs. Ingalls presiding at the organ.

Prayer followed by Rev. Phebe A. Hanaford—a prayer of dedication, and an expression of thanksgiving for the fulfillment thus far of the cherished hopes of many in regard to a place of worship at Siasconset, and also an utterance of gratitude that the occasion was one free from the sorrow which was narrowly escaped, and full of the gladness which the remembrance of the unbroken circles could but give. At the close of this prayer, the hymn 'Jesus, Lover of my Soul' was sung. Mr. J. Ormond Wilson, superintendent of schools in Washington, D. C., then read the following:

"Miss Garrison desires to express publicly her gratitude for her rescue from death: first to God, then to the Rev. Dr. Johnson, who so nobly went to her rescue and brought her to land, and to the more than brave lady, his wife, who, entirely forgetful of herself, urged her husband forward in the face of death; then to the ladies who so ably and tenderly brought her back to consciousness and health; and particularly to Miss Tissington and Mrs. Burbank, without whose aid she would hardly have recovered; and finally, gratitude and acknowledgments go to the whole people of Siasconset, for their interest and many manifestations of regard and kindness."

Rev. Mrs. Hanaford then addressed the assembly. Referring to the matter for special thanksgiving which was in all hearts, she presented, with fitting language, a beautiful wreath formed of grasses and 'life-everlasting'—(emblems of the gospel Mr. Johnson is called to preach, and which he nobly exemplified by his heroic act,) to Mrs. Johnson for her husband, expressing the admiration of all for the union of self-sacrifice, which made the wife urge her husband to a service he was so ready to perform, both knowing that in that angry sea his life also would be imperilled. (The wreath was made by Miss Ellen E. Miles of Jersey City, to whom the credit of this pleasing episode in the service

5

belongs.) Mrs. Johnson gracefully received it, and at
the close of Mrs. Hanaford's address responded with an
audible 'Amen.'

"The speaker then went on to refer to the fact that
all hearts were united in gratitude to those whose generosity had secured this piece of land for future use as
the ground for a Union Chapel, and closed with the
following lines, written by her for the occasion:

We dedicate to Him who is 'Our Father'—
  The Friend and Father of each human soul—
This plot of ground whereon to-night we gather,
  With glad emotions we can scarce control.

Rev'rent we bow, with but one common feeling
  Of deep thanksgiving that those lives are spared,
So lately to our sympathies appealing,—
  The one in peril,* and the one who dared.†

Wildly the waves upon our white sands breaking,
  May send abroad their ceaseless, solemn tones,
But we, the echoes of the heart awaking,
  Sound our *Te Deum* for the rescued ones.

And when, in days to come, Thy children gather—
  Of every name, in one dear Name made one,—
Within the temple here to stand, Our Father,
  May praises rise in union as begun !

---

* Miss Garrison, who was swept off by the surf.
† Rev. G. D. Johnson, who risked his own life to save a drowning stranger.

And thou, Great Helper! then, as now and ever,
  Give all the victory in each trying hour,
Till safe, where no dividing waves may sever,
  They stand, death-freed, upon the heavenly shore.

"Rev. George D. Johnson of New Brighton, S. I., then read the *Te Deum* and several appropriate collects to which the proper responses were made, and the interesting services closed with singing of 'All hail the power of Jesus' name,' and the benediction by Rev. Mr. Johnson.

"It will be seen that the first service on this ground was thus a union service, ministers of two denominations being present, and all hearts united in sentiments of thanksgiving and Christian fellowship and good-will."

The invalid laid aside the newspaper article with the remark that she was not surprised at the satisfaction she so often heard expressed in reference to the Chapel, and thought that only Quakers, or those who like them had learned to worship everywhere, and on all days, could have endured so long the absence of a place in which to gather for outward expression of worship.

And the invalid was right.

CHAPTER VII.

CHATTING BY THE SEA.

"Thy charms, Siasconset, no one can describe,
    Or the pleasure we take as we thitherward ride;
The calm, sunny wave and the deep, heaving sea,
    Are both emblematic, dear 'Sconset, of thee."

LYDIA BARNEY.

"OME," said the invalid, now as ready to seek the beach as any of the 'Sconset visitors, "isn't it most time for our little reading by the vast and lonely sea?" This expression "vast and lonely sea" had been heard so often from the same lips, in description, or in admiration, or as an exclamation, that not infrequently it provoked a smile, which she good-naturedly observed, and with an answering smile, as if repetition settled the value of the phrase, repeated it again. Ultimately it became only necessary to say "vast and lonely," with a questioning or beseeching tone, and it was understood, hats and shawls or parasols secured, and the steps turned seaward.

So beside "the vast and lonely," the N. M. and the invalid were soon sitting, one reading aloud in "Ben Hur," that wondrously attractive first chapter where the three camels and their unique riders appear upon the lonely desert, the other listening with eyes fixed upon the wide and rolling main, but thoughts far away in the land where history was born.

By-and-by a lady stranger, who was often there on the shore at an early hour, from love of the beach and its attractions, came within sound of the well-chosen words of Gen. Wallace, and asked the privilege of remaining to listen. Of course it was granted, and now that wonderful book can never be read by those ladies without a pleasant association with the sandy shore and the "vast and lonely sea."

The energetic Helen, having attended to the comfort of all the household, at last appeared upon the beach, and soon after the bathers began to gather also. The admitted listener departed, and the trio sat conversing and gazing, in a sweet restfulness peculiar to that hour and place.

They were not far from the rude steps, and sloping pathway, which the public generally used, and the crowd always gathered about the rope at that place. Tents were there also, and chairs, and not far away on

the sands, some old fish houses, and some houses for
bathers to use for dressing. Away to the north there
was another rope, and the dwellers on Sunset Heights
mainly used that place for bathing. It was however
considered less safe than the first and most frequented
one.

And while the trio sat and gazed, they talked. The
more dangerous spot for bathers came in for a share of
attention, and Helen told her that one morning—the very
morning when " the Death Angel flapped his dark wing
o'er the wave," but finally passed on without taking the
fair young girl—she was on the beach, with a little niece
of the family, who usually bathed close to the shore,
but as the waves were rough, simply waded on the edge
of the surf holding fast to the rope far up from the spot
where the breakers rose and fell. " Soon we perceived,"
said Helen, " that there was consternation among the
older bathers. We turned our eyes from the little girl
we were watching, and saw that many were rushing
towards one spot on the beach, by the northern rope.
There was a shouting and frantic motions. Strong
men left the ocean where they were bathing and ran
swiftly along the beach. Women followed. Children
also began to go. I left Lillian to the care of her aunt,
and started." " Yes," said the N. M. " and I rose from

the shawl on which I was seated, gathered up said
shawl, with Lillian's clothes in it, and bidding her run
also, in her bathing suit, I made the best of my way
there, but Helen far outstripped me. When I arrived,
Helen was walking beside the board on which the half-
drowned girl was stretched, and called to me for the
shawl, in which Lillian's clothes were borne along.
Clothing, shoes, everything, was dropped on the hot
sand, and the shawl was spread over the wet form of
the unconscious teacher, and stout men bore her on,
while I gathered up the dropped articles, and, accompanied by the little niece, followed along. While the
indefatigable Helen, and others in Major Burbank's
cottage, were resuscitating the rescued one, I dressed the
wet and shivering child, and then joined the women in
the little bed-room, and rubbed the cold feet, while
some faithful worker rested a moment from her benevo-
lent effort. That gave me the opportunity to see what
I never saw before, nor since, the return of a spirit to
this world, when it had been long unconscious, and
there was danger that it would never revive in the flesh
again. It was a glad yet solemn hour, and the voice of
the young girl was as a sound from the far shore of a
vast eternity. She had risen up on the board with a
sort of convulsive effort, as they brought her over the

beach, opened her eyes, gazed around as if in farewell, laid back and never moved again, till she spoke in the query as to whether she was in the spirit land or not."

"That was a narrow escape?" remarked the invalid. "She was drifting far out toward the Silent Sea," answered the N. M., "when they cut those tent-ropes with which to attempt a rescue." "What tent-ropes?" "Why, after her rescuer had reached the big bather's rope with her, and was holding on there, and supporting her, it was necessary for him to have help, he was so exhausted, so they cut the tent-ropes, and threw to him, and he fastened the rope about her, so that they were both drawn in together. A board was used sometimes by the family which owned a large dog, when he played with them in the breakers, but the noble fellow was not at hand that day to join in the rescue. His board, however, served as a litter on which to bear the rescued one to the sheltering love and care which gave rich evidence of the sympathetic heart of Siasconset."

"Then you think Siasconset is not given over to fashion and folly, yet, even though it has begun to be a watering-place?" continued the invalid.

"Heart, indeed!" exclaimed the impetuous Helen, "if you had seen all I have seen, and known the ins and outs of families here, you would say there was little

danger of any failure to obtain sympathy in any needed
direction. Siasconset has a noble, brave and generous
heart, people with brains come here to rest the head,
but neither they nor the natives intend to be hard-
hearted or icebergs."

"I can answer for many of the natives," added the
N. M., "that they can appreciate, and would not hesitate
to adopt, Tuckerman's words :

> 'Give me the boon of love !
>   I ask no more for fame ;
> Far better one unpurchased heart
>   Than glory's proudest name.
>
> *　　　*　　　*　　　*
>
> Give me the boon of love !
>   The lamp of fame shines far,
> But love's soft light glows near and warm—
>   A pure and household star.'

The natives are glad to have such visitors as are now
drawn here, and hope that the island will always be
attractive to such, who have hearts as well as heads, and
noble purposes in life whether their purses are heavy
or not."

"But tell me, Helen," asked the invalid, "how came
you to get that wreath for the noble rescuer?"

"That wreath came to crown the victor of its own
accord, so to speak," responded Helen, "for George

took us to ride that afternoon over toward Tom Nevers,
and as we loitered on the way and gathered flowers, I
found some shiny silver button and some meadow grasses
to add to my bouquet.   After we got home, the idea of
a wreath that would not fade, at once came to my mind,
and I selected the grasses, whose language is 'consola-
tion,' and the silver button, you know, is often called
'life-everlasting.'   They seemed appropriate—they could
be preserved—and I used them.   I hope they are still in
that wreath to-day, and that the wreath is as full of
pleasant association to him who received it, as it was to
me when I made it."

"Did you see the lady he rescued, again, after she was
recovered?" inquired the invalid.

"Yes, indeed!   She was a teacher in the city of
Washington, you know; and the superintendent of
Washington schools was here with his family at the
time.   He and his wife would not let her go back to the
hotel, after the sad experience, but took her to their own
cottage, and there I saw her; she was lying on the bed
at 'Hearts-Ease' Cottage.   I can seem to see her now, with
that pretty, blue jacket on, and a bunch of daisies at her
belt.   No more hotel meals for her.   No more loneli-
ness.   She was as if at home.   There again was the
heart of Siasconset seen ; for the Wilsons were su c

frequent visitors that they and 'Sconset seemed to have adopted each other. Many a time have the 'Sconseters seen Mr. Wilson with his bag of 'penny shells,' wending his way home from Low Beach, and all were pleased who knew why they were gathered and saved."

"Why, what *could* he do with them?" and the invalid's handsome eyes opened wide as she asked the question.

"He took them to Washington," said Helen, "and gave them to the children of the primary schools who were learning arithmetic, and could use them in adding and subtracting."

"How admirable!" exclaimed the invalid, whose many years of successful teaching enabled her to appreciate his wise fore-thought.

"Do you remember what Miss Garrison said to you, Helen?" asked the N. M.

"Oh, yes! When I asked her if she would ever go in bathing again, she said she should like to try it another summer, to show Siasconset that she had no ill-will against it or its treacherous surf."

"There spoke the brave and noble spirit!" said the invalid. "She was worthy to be an object of sympathy and tender interest in the heart of Siasconset. Have you ever seen her since?"

" Yes, in Washington, once, and her beloved mother
was with her; a pleasing gentlewoman so precious to the
daughter that she thoughtfully begged those who were
near her at the time of her peril and rescue, not to let
the incident get into the papers, lest the dear mother
might hear of it and be affected in health by the
thought of her child's peril."

"Do you wonder," asked the N. M. of the invalid,
" that we listened with unusual interest to the hymn :

'Jesus, lover of my soul.'

on that night following her danger, and thought of the
hero also as we remembered how 'the nearer waters
rolled' in that awful period of suspense and effort?"

" And how that magnificent voice of Mr. Brooks rose
and fell in the cadences of the familiar hymn, while the
tears rained down many cheeks, as they gratefully
thought of the danger and deliverance!" added Helen,
"Oh, Jean, you should hear him! And you will hear
him when the little Chapel is dedicated. His generous
heart will be recognised in the thrilling tones of that
inspiring voice."

And thus they talked, changing the theme from time
to time, till the last bather rushed up the sands toward
the dry clothing, and the last acquaintance greeted ·
them that morning by " the vast and lonely sea."

CHAPTER VIII.

SESACHACHA.

"They called the pond Sesachacha,
  Whatever that may mean,
I only know the fairies dwelt
  Above its silver sheen.

* * * * * *

A blessing on the fairy pond,
  The oars that, glinting, swing,
Where cliffs re-echo, soft and low,
  The songs we used to sing!"

EUNICE B. LAMBERTON.

O look across to the 'Ocean View,' Helen! the steps are full of people, and there are pleasure wagons, and, I verily believe, fishing-poles, and where *can* they be going?" exclaimed the invalid, a part of whose pleasure consisted in keeping her lovely eyes wide open for all the new sights, and her mind alert to add always to its store.

"Shall I run across and inquire?" was the humorous

response of the busy Helen, who could usually guess at what others would make effort to learn, and her guess would be equal to their study, often-times.

"Oh, no!" laughed her sister, "I think I shall survive even if I don't find out, but I do believe they are going pond-fishing. Are there any ponds or brooks around here?"

"I know," said the N. M. hastening to air her superior knowledge, "they are going to 'Sachacha."

"And where is that, pray?"

"You wouldn't ask, Jean, if you remembered Northrup's 'Chapter ix' as you do Childe Harold's Cantos, for he gives a glowing picture of his Squantum at 'Sachacha Pond."

"A squantum? oh yes—a sort of picnic."

"A picnic with pond-fishing thrown in!" interjected Helen.

"Do let me get the book and read what the genial 'Squire says"—and away the N. M. sped to the sitting-room where ''Sconset Cottage Life' had an honored place upon the table, with the albums and autograph books of various sizes.

Then she read the charming and truthful description, as follows:

"What a delightful ride that was! Out beyond the

town into the fenceless fields, over the swelling waves
of the landscape, through little vales and over the ridges
and around the mounds :—skirting little emerald ponds
no bigger than a village door-yard and surrounded by
wild shrubbery, golden-rod and flaming flowers;—out
among the heather, the dwarf oaks no higher than your
knee, the creeping meal-berry vines with hard, red fruit,
like beads, the low, huckleberry bushes tempting you
to dismount over the seat and back-step ; winding and
turning and following the parallel ruts wherever they
led ; at length coming to a gate and a vast sheep-pas-
ture, and letting ourselves through and carefully closing
the gate after us ; catching gleams of the sea now and
then on our right, and on our left looking up with
respect on the low range of Saul's Hills as being the
highest land in all Nantucket; at length by a swoop
and a turn coming down from the west upon a bay of
'Sachacha Pond, our 'Squantum-ground.'

A small, deserted house, surrounded by soft, luxuri-
ant turf, green and inviting, made the objective point
which all pleasure seeking requires, while the adjacent
barn ministered comfort and protection to our horses
from the August sun. After descending from our
vehicles and bestowing edibles and extra apparel under
a broad, extemporized awning, we strolled down to the

bay. A thirty foot whale-boat, propelled by two small
boys, leisurely approached, and the round dozen of us
embarked and slowly moved out into the lake, to the
edge of the shallow water, where for half an hour in a
most juvenile fashion, and in high glee, we fished for
perch—that being strictly typical of the legitimate
squantum in this particular locality.*

" Now I understand it all," said the invalid, as the N.
M. ceased reading, "and the next thing to be done is
to live it all out. I suppose we also can go to Sach—
what do you call it ?"

" Sesachacha, is the name—'Sachacha, for short,"
replied the N. M., and Helen added,

" Get strong, Jean, as fast as you can, and we will get
the boys—I mean Robert and George—to carry us over,
all hands, and we'll gather huckleberries and pond-fish
at the same time."

But they never did. They went in sight of 'Sachacha
Pond, however. How blue and beautiful the little lake
appeared! That was a glorious, summer day, when
Robert, the elder brother of the N. M., drew up his nice,
spring wagon before the door, and Helen mounted to
his side on the front seat, while the invalid and the N.
M. filled the back one. Off they went, receiving a

---

* Northrop's "'Sconset Cottage Life," p. 78.

pleasant greeting as they passed George's door, where
Mary Eliza waved her "good bye." On, over the hill,
along the grassy roads, through the gates, up to Sancoty Head. "Oh, what a glorious view!" exclaimed
the invalid, and then sat in rapt silence gazing on the
broad, blue ocean in front, the eye sweeping the horizon
for snowy sails, and often gratified. Far away stretched
the white and curving beach, and in the distance rose
dimly to view the tall tower of the light-house at Great
Point.

"Did you ever go there?" asked the invalid.

"Yes," answered the N. M., "once, and only once in
all my life, and that was in my half-century year. If I
had been born a boy I know I would not have waited so
long as that, for, from early childhood I had desired to
go there, having been stimulated to do so, by the story
often told me, of my own mother's delight, when in her
childhood, she was a visitor for a day to the far-off
light-house, fifteen or more miles from town. That
mother died in my infancy, you know, but any thing
which she enjoyed had a romantic charm for me. I
wished to live over her pleasant experiences. But I
never did, till, in a North-East storm, one August, my
brother George took me in his covered wagon, with a
buffalo robe about us to keep us warm. A dear friend

6

O Sancoty ! send thy bright flashes afar !—p. 52.

From Harper's Magazine.—Copyright, 1873, by Harper & Brothers.

who desired to observe the botany of that region, (she being, moreover, the lady President of the Botanical Society, whom you have met,) accompanied us, and my nephew, Lawrence, walked the whole way—ten miles— from 'Sconset, to meet us there, and learn from her about the flora of that sandy point."

"Was it worth while?" asked the invalid, languidly.

"Indeed it was worth while, to us all, and when you want to see a sample of the coarser sand on that beach, which seems so far away, come to my home, and seek for a large, glass jar of it, which stands upon the revolving book-case in my study."

"Among other useless trash!" exclaimed Helen, playfully, yet with a look at the white stone set in a ring upon her finger, (which quartz pebble came from Fire Island beach, where Margaret Fuller was shipwrecked), that proved she was not unmindful of the value given to inanimate things by association with the life of a human being, or the memory of red-letter days.

The party in the wagon alighted, and sat for a while upon a bench near the edge of the grassy bank. Steep and bare was the sandy cliff, as they looked over the edge, and far below them was the white and narrow beach, with the surf gently breaking on the shore, so gently that the sound scarce rose to their ears. It was a

perfect, summer morning! As rare as any June day!
And the memory of it lingers with every one of that
party as a sweet expression of the divine peace. Instinctively the conversation turned upon the presence of
God in Nature, and there was expressed a holy gladness
in the thought that the True and the Beautiful are one
with the Good, and that mortals may expect the descent
of power to grow in usefulness and excellence, as they
lift, in aspiring sincerity, the prayer of the Psalmist,
" Let the beauty of the Lord our God be upon us, and
establish Thou the work of our hands, yea, the work of
our hands establish Thou it!" That prayer can only be
truly prayed by those whose work is beneficent, and who
have learned how to serve God by serving humanity.

The summons to return to the village came all too
soon; but the kind brother had many cares, and the little
leisure for the ride had all been used. Reluctantly
they turned their backs on 'Sachacha and Sancoty.
Quietly they rode along till they met a little boy, who
pleasantly opened a gate for them, and after closing it,
rewarded himself by a ride. Standing on the iron step
of the wagon, he held fast to the back of the seat, upon
which sat the invalid and the N. M. Opening her sun-
umbrella for comfortable shade, the N. M. suddenly became oblivious to all that occurred, and to this day is

unable to recall the swift-following events. Evidently
the horse perceived the motion of the opening, jumped
forward and ran, the little boy was jerked off the step;
he clung, naturally, to the seat—it was not fastened!—
and over went backward those who were upon it, strik-
ing on the back of the head, and losing consciousness
for a brief season.

The horse dashed forward, and the driver sought to
control him. Helen looked round, and saw no back
seat, no companions! Where were the sister and friend!
Quick as thought, frantic with fear, as she saw two im-
movable forms upon the ground behind her, Helen
leaped over the seat and out of the wagon, while Robert
quieted the horse, and then hastily returned to the
scene of the catastrophe. The N. M. was struggling to
rise, declaring she was unhurt, when her brother reached
her. He put his arms around her and kissed her, in
joy that she was yet alive, but with no little anxiety as
he perceived her incoherent and rapid speech.

The invalid had whispered to her sister, "Helen, I
am killed," but the undaunted Helen, to whom the
knowledge that instant death had not come to her dear
ones seemed as an inspiration for effort in their behalf,
soon had her upon her feet, and with the brother's help,
had both the injured ones in the wagon, and they rapid-

ly sought their cottage home.   As they passed the door
from whence was waved the cordial greeting, the un-
wonted position of the ladies on the floor of the wagon,
awoke surprise and anxiety.   " Something has happened
to them!" said George and his wife, and the dinner-table
was left at once that help might be rendered, if needful.

Then was the heart of Siasconset seen again.   Not
only relatives, but neighbors, and strangers came to
render aid.   The invalid was placed upon a bed, the
N. M. on a lounge, and for a little season the sympathy
of the village flowed toward Coffyn Cottage, and its inmates.   Even a lady physician of Wellesley College
came with her medical aid, and though she has since
changed her name on receiving a wedding ring, yet the
hearts of her patients will always cherish that of Dr.
Emily Jones.

The accident proved to have no very serious result,
and after a few days, the ladies who had thus uncere-
moniously left the wagon, were as well as ever.   But
they had learned how sympathetic 'Sconset folks and
their visitors could be.   Flowers, fruit, and dainty
dishes—even little 'Sconset birds prepared with culi-
nary art—evinced that sympathy, and loving words,
written and spoken, are laid up in the archives of grateful memories.

It was a day long to be remembered. The N. M. can never forget the venerable father, with his anxious look, listening to her incoherent speech, and rapid questioning, while tears filled the eyes of the brother who had meant to give his sister a pleasant outing, and was distressed at such an ending of the ride; and the invalid will long remember the devotion of Helen to her comfort, the long night when she watched anxiously lest the accident might make the invalid despair of ever realizing health again, and all the many evidences that though she saw Sesachacha only afar off, she felt the beating of the heart of Siasconset very near.

CHAPTER IX.

SUNSET GLORY.

" I stood on Siasconset's hill,
    Just at the set of sun,
Aud looked abroad o'er that fair plain,
    And down by Philip's run.
The kine were winding o'er the lea,
    And, far as eye could reach,
The sheep were feeding quietly,
    From Plainfield to Low Beach."

GEORGE HOWLAND FOLGER.

HAT lovely sunsets we have on Nantucket!" ex-claimed Helen, one night, as she sat on the low step at the front door of Coffyn Cottage, and saw the visitors, men and women, singly or in groups, some-times two only, whispering low, and arm in arm, (one could easily fancy them lovers), walking up New Street toward the hill, which seemed the village boundary on the west."

" Why not go to the top of the hill, with the rest of

of the people?" suggested the N. M. "Jean can read
Carlyle, by Froude, and we'll study Nature."

Jean did not object, for she knew that if she did not
care to be wearied by the walk to the hill-top, she could
yet enjoy much of the wonderful glory which was so
often all abroad at the sunset hour.

So, arm in arm, Helen and the N. M. strolled toward
the western hill-top, and, when there, stood in rapturous amazement, at the glory of the heavens, and the
wide landscape spread beneath. Familiarity could not
make this gorgeous sunset common. Like Truth, however old, it was forever fresh. To lovers of the Beautiful it was untiringly welcome. The clouds were glowing with the most brilliant sunset hues, so rich in tint
and blazing in light, as to be utterly indescribable;
poetry even failed to present their beauty of coloring,
and "radiancy of glory,"—and the pencil of a Claude
would fail to reproduce it. No wonder the summer
visitors, and such of the villagers as were not too busy
with the "chores," flocked to the summit of the hill
whereon the school-house stood, to view the wonderful
display of sunset glory as fully as possible.

Nor was it strange that the N. M. repeated the lines
at the head of this chapter, and so praised the whole
poem, and the Nantucketer who wrote it, that on their

return the little book compiled by Miss Lucy C. Star-buck, entitled "Seaweeds from the Shores of Nantucket," was taken up, and the poem read aloud in the sonorous voice and characteristic manner of the elocutionist—Helen. When it was read, and the history of the island, and especially of the two Indian tribes who inhabited it before the white race came, had been freely commented on, the N. M. expressed her special satisfaction with the two following stanzas, which she read aloud with an energy of manner and the depth of tone which proved her pride of ancestry; and her interest in all that concerned the special glory of Nantucket, or won for the dear island, in any sense, the respect and applause of posterity.

> " Our pilgrim-fathers forth were driven
>   By persecution's rod,
> And sought this isle among the waves,
>   Where they could worship God.
> When autumn's clouds lowered in the sky,
>   Old Thomas dared the sea,
> With Edward nobly by his side,
>   They'd die or they'd be free.
>
> They were a race of giant-souls,
>   Of stout and stalwart forms ;
> In boyhood rocked upon the waves,
>   And cradled in the storms.

They bore our country's flag aloft,
In battle and in breeze,
The first to show its rebel stars
Within Old England's seas."

"Were Nantucketers really the first to bear the flag we all love so well to Great Britain?" asked Jean.

"So it seems," answered the N. M., "according to a statement in Godfrey's 'Guide.'"

"Ho! that may not be correct," exclaimed the out-spoken Helen, "for Godfrey declares you to be born at 'Sconset, and your memory doesn't agree with his statement!"

"My father has been so long here at 'Sconset," remarked the N. M., "that I suppose Mr. Godfrey thought all of his children must have been born here, whereas only the youngest was—and I am the oldest."

"Well—where were you born?" asked Jean.

"In town—in Hussey Street, Nantucket. Lower Hussey Street, we called it, and grandfather used to laughingly say he owned all the houses in the street. The 'all' was but one, and in that one both my father and myself were born. The house belonged to my father's grandfather, Nathaniel Coffin, and when my father was a baby—over eighty years ago—the house stood where now the Ocean House stands.

"Nothing like knowing all about one's birth-place and ancestry," playfully responded Helen, "but I want to know about the flag."

"Well, Helen, let me read you this paragraph on Godfrey's 338 page: "At the earliest moment after peace had been declared, when safety rendered it expedient, the ship 'Bedford,' Capt. William Mooers, with a load of four hundred and eighty-seven butts of oil, was despatched to London, and to this ship belongs the honor of having been the first vessel to hoist the American flag in any British port.' And a note says: 'F. C. Sanford, Esq., informs the compiler that this was Feb. 3, 1783; and that she arrived at Nantucket from London, May 31, 1783, her entry at the custom house at the time being in his possession. Does'nt that sound 'all correct on the right,' Helen?"

"Oh yes, and 'all correct on the left,' too; but jt is all back of our memory, and who cares about it anyway!" replied Helen, who cared more for the gorgeous beauty of the sunset hour, or the brilliant coloring and fairy forms of the wild flowers everywhere blooming in the vicinity of 'Sconset, than she did for all the ancestral legends in the world; and while she was an admirable teacher of history, she was a yet more enthusiastic student of botany. Hence her reply.

But the N. M. was not stirred in spirit. She kept on thinking of the far-off days. "Why my father's father was only seven years old then! There were only a little over four thousand people on the whole island, and they were about building Great Point Light-house. There were no public schools for forty years after that."

"What will you say when I remind you that *twice* in Godfrey's book, you are mentioned as being a native of 'Sconset?" said Helen, who had become somewhat weary of a matter that had been often mentioned in somewhat irate fashion by the N. M.

"Do! what can I do, but say he didn't know any better, and so excuse him?" replied the N. M.

"I rather think," said Jean, quietly, "that you had better call to mind the difficulties you have found yourself when writing of people and things, and while you bemoan your own inaccuracies in what you desired to be correct statements, because of your own insufficient knowledge or erroneous information, you had better forgive poor Godfrey. I don't believe he meant to make incorrect statements."

"Neither do I, pacific Jean!" responded the N. M., "and I will forgive him, but I shall set the matter right, all the same."

"All-e-samee!" laughed Helen, "and we'll call our dear invalid, 'Jean, the Pacificator!'"

Then the conversation went back to the Indians, and
all were interested, as by reference to various author-
ities they learned that only ten years after the Pilgrim
fathers landed, occurred a war between the Indian tribes
of the East and West parts of the island; the last war
that occurred here, and the only one of which we have
any knowledge.   The island was then largely covered
with forest trees, most of which were oaks.   Some of the
oldest houses on the island, and notably the old chapel,
or vestry, of the North Church, was built of island wood.

"Yes, you two school-ma'ams," said the N. M., "had
better whet up your memories concerning history, for
it was only twenty-one years after the Pilgrims landed
that this island was deeded to Thomas Mayhew by Lord
Sterling."

"Who *assumed* the right to do so !" sharply suggested
the keen-eyed Helen.

"Mayhew felt he had power to sell the property at
any rate, from that deed, and so," said the N. M. "he
passed it over to my ancestors in 1659—which was
thirty-nine years after the Mayflower came."

"I thought you were going to say some of your ancestors came over in the Mayflower," laughed Helen.

"Perhaps they did," replied the N. M., nothing
daunted ; "for was not the pilot of the Mayflower named
Robert Coffin ?"

"I might have known you would have found a connection some way," added Helen.

The N. M. smiled, and went on to say, "Eighty
pounds and two beaver hats, was not a large price to
give, for this delightful island."

"That depends!" exclaimed Helen, "let's see. £80 =
$400! Well, it's worth all that now, any how, and your
ancestors coming here made it worth visiting."

"Yes, you need not laugh, Helen. People have
always liked to visit Nantucket. It has had not only
Governors and Presidents, but a royal visitor, for King
Philip was here in 1665."

"How long after the Pilgrims landed?" roguishly
asked Helen.

"Well, forty-five years," answered the N. M., "but
now I'll thank you to cease asking that question, for
I'll date in future from the coming of Pilgrims Thomas
Macy and Edward Starbuck, and Chief Magistrate Tristram Coffyn, and Interpreter Peter Folger, and Thomas
Barnard and Christopher Hussey, Thomas Coleman,
and the Swains, and the rest of the original purchasers
and their associates." It was fifteen years after the
island belonged to my ancestors before the warlike chief
came. And he came in no pacific spirit. His hostile
appearance made the inhabitants apprehensive, for the

English were few in number, and ill prepared to meet a foreign foe."

"Of course he didn't come for his health, as I did," said the invalid, "what induced him to dare the dangerous wave in his canoe? He couldn't have had any other craft."

"You are right about the mode of transit," replied the N. M., "he and his fellow-warriors came in canoes, in pursuit of an Indian they wished to punish. And what do you suppose was the culprit's offence?"

"Perhaps he was thievish," quickly answered Helen, "as many Indians are."

"Thieves are not all of Indian blood," continued the N. M., "but this man had broken no moral law. He had only set at naught an Indian custom."

"Was that enough to rouse a king?" exclaimed Jean.

"It was the king himself who had been dishonored by the mention of his father's name," responded the N. M. "Let me read you what Obed Macy says about it in his 'History of Nantucket.'"

So the N. M. sought the volume and then read as follows: "Rehearsing the name of the dead, if it should be that of a distinguished person, was decreed by the natives a very high crime, for which nothing but the life of the culprit could atone. Philip, having now the

poor criminal in possession, made preparations to execute vengeance upon him, when the English spectators,
commiserated his condition, and made offers of money
to ransom his life. Philip listened to these offers and
mentioned a sum which would satisfy him; but so much
could not be collected. He was informed of this, but
would not lessen his demand. The whites, however,
collected all they could, in the short time allowed them,
in hopes that he would be satisfied, when assured that
more could not be found; but instead of this, he persisted in his demand with threatening language, pro-
nounced with an emphasis which foreboded no good.
This very much provoked the English, so that they concluded among themselves to make no farther offers, but
try to frighten him away without giving him any more
money. The sum raised, which was all that the inhabitants possessed, was eleven pounds; this had already
been paid to him, and could not be required back again.
Philip had surrounded, and taken possession of, one or
two houses, to the great terror of the inmates; in this
dilemma they concluded to put all to risk; they told
him, that, if he did not immediately leave the island,
they would rally the inhabitants, and fall upon him and
cut him off to a man. Not knowing their defenceless
condition, he happily took the alarm, and left the

7

island as soon as possible.   The prisoner was then set at
liberty."

Helen laughed heartily over "the bluster of the
whites," as she termed it, and the question arose whether
King Philip was cowardly or mercenary, and finally
decided that he was both; but all justified the whites in
seeking to buy the life of the poor man, and all rejoiced
that the Indians of the island had forever passed away.
The civilization of later days could not harmonize with
their primitive habits and crude ideas, and there seems
to be no room in this busy life of the nineteenth century
for these so-called children of Nature.

"Did you ever see any of the Nantucket Indians?"
asked Jean of the N. M.

"No," was the reply, "for every full-blooded Indian
was gone, I suppose, before I arrived.   In 1764 there
was a sort of plague which swept away over two-hun-
dred, and there were left only 136, it is said, and they
faded and failed, till, in my childhood, there was only
one man with Indian blood in his veins—and he died
about 1855.   I saw him several times, and once conversed a little with him.   He was gentle and courteous,
as I remember.   There's a good portrait of him in the
Nantucket Atheneum."

A little more conversation about Abram Quary (or

Quady) and then the ripple of chat was suddenly stopped
in its quiet flow, as callers entered, and the short summer evening had reached bed-time when they again
crossed the threshold of the cottage, with their cheery
" Good night and pleasant dreams!"

CHAPTER X.

SUNRISE AT SIASCONSET.

"Loved sea-girt isle! the murmuring waves,
 And stern old ocean's ceaseless roar,
Bring back to mind such memories dear
 Of days, when, on thy pebbly shore,
Our childish feet have wandered far
 In search of treasures from the sea:
We recked not of the world beyond
 Such sweet content we found in thee!"

MRS. MARGARET **G. LaForge.**

I'T was the morning hour—not "a morning without
 clouds," but one when the light, fleecy clouds were
just tinted with color, and finally illumed with glory,
when Helen sought the beach alone. She had been
wakeful all the night previous, and listened with un-
speakably solemn, yet sweet, emotions, to the low murmur of the surf. At times there would come the longer,
louder roll which betokened a larger wave which had
found its rest; a wave started in some far-off storm-
swept sea to find the final pause upon that island shore.

As the morning dawned, she softly rose and dressed for the beach, then, slipping out gently from the back door of the cottage, she quietly threaded the little passage-ways, called, by courtesy, "streets," and was soon upon the brow of the hill above the spot where the boats were drawn up on the beach.

All was silent in that early hour of the summer morning, save the incessant murmur of the heaving sea as it gently touched the sandy shore. No sign of life except that restless ocean, and the sea-gull sweeping along above some crested wave. She descended by the stony pathway, trod the planks, and soon found herself beside the surf which lapped lazily the long, white beach. It was an hour fitted for solemn communion with the Highest and Holiest. An hour for praise! An hour for reverent awe, and wondering delight! Unanswered queries arose in her mind. Unanswerable questions formulated themselves, on the lips which ever and anon opened to utter the sublime ascriptions of the ancient Psalmist:

"The sea is His and He made it."

"The Lord on high is mightier than the noise of many waters."

But there was no response from Nature, save with Nature's voices, to the eye and ear, viz.: the rippling

wave of the summer surf, and the distant cry of the
whirling sea-bird, as he skimmed along above the waves
now glinting in the morning sunlight. The beauty of
that hour was impressive. So was the silence. It
brought the Presence close to the soul of Helen, and
she repeated—

> "The Infinite always is silent,
>   It is only the Finite speaks,
>   Our words are the idle wave-caps
>   On the deep that never breaks.
> We may question with words of science—
>   Explain, decide and discuss,
>   But only in meditation
>   The mystery speaks to us."*

Thus she lingered by the side of the ocean, till, after
a long, quiet, restful period, the form of a human being
was perceived upon the bank. He drew nearer and was
recognized as a fisherman, who proceeded at once to his
little dory, which he drew to the water side, and putting
into it the bait and hooks, he launched it and himself
out on the broad, peaceful waters, to procure the finny
treasures that would secure him warm welcome from
the villagers when he returned.

"Horace has gone out for blue-fish!" was the report

---

* John Boyle O'Reilly.

of Helen, when she at last returned to Coffyn Cottage, and found the old Captain ' on deck,' as he said, and the fire started for breakfast.

Domestic duties followed, and while the invalid after the early meal, had donned her scarlet wrapper, and gone out to see the lady of ladies—"Cousin Eliza"—the son of that lady, whose graphic speech and witty sentences were often quoted, made a brief call on Helen and the rest of the family. The N. M. was "in town;" the children gone out to play; the aged sea-captain was sunning himself on the bench in front of the house, and Helen was priding herself on having "improved the time," and gone ahead of all competitors, having, as she exultingly told the " Professor " and " Joseph," when they called, hung one hundred pieces on the line. For the "Professor" had come up from town with his family and friends, including the venerable, cheery, beloved grandmother, who was already quite far along in the nineties, and he was evidently a little annoyed at finding Helen at the wash-tub—an exultant piece of in-dependence—rather than dressed and ready for the pic-nic party on the beach.

"Never mind, Robert," exclaimed she, "just leave your things here, and let me all alone, and when the time comes, you come for the coffee, and I will be all ready, and go with you."

And go she did. The early, morning walk had proved
an inspiration. She had worked with a will, and the
neatly dressed lady, who was greeted with loud hand-
clapping and shouts as she appeared upon the beach—
was able to exult over a fair day's work as she sat down
to dinner on the sandy shore, with as "goodlie a com-
panie" of scholarly and cultured and intelligent men
and women as ever trod old 'Sconset beach. It does not
detract from one's social position at 'Sconset if the head
and hands are alike busy at the call of duty. The heart
of Siasconset is in sympathy with Him who said, "My
Father worketh hitherto and I work," and they are
especially respected whose kind efforts help the weary
ones to rest; removing the burden of care from those
they love, and bearing it bravely with a strong and
patient heart. She, who was the honored of all in that
little, picnic party by the sea, had not wasted her ninety
and more years in idleness. Head, heart, and hands
had been busy for scores of years, for children and grandchildren, and at that advanced period in her life there
were great-great-grandchildren to rise up and call her
blessed. Merry laugh and pleasant speech; kindly advice and brilliant repartee; harmless gossip and neighborly talk : with the spices of literary criticism, and
scholastic lore occasionally, made the sea-side party

memorable to all who were there ; one of whom looks
back upon it now from amidst the still more gladsome
assemblage on the shining shore. Old age is not known
beyond the river. The mind, when freed from the body,
displays its own everlasting youth.

But even sea-shore parties must come to a close, and
long before sunset the company was scattered, Coffyn
Cottage received its accustomed number, and the others
in their great beach-wagon rumbled up New Lane,
reached the hill top, rode along in *silhouette* against the
western horizon and then sank behind the hill, a merry
party still, upon the road to town.

There were frequent callers at the cottage. One welcome couple came—the lame and the blind—but there
was no halting in the steps which the spirit took as one
of them walked along the pleasant paths of poetry,
and no failure of vision as the other took the glass of
faith and looked away to the delectable mountains.
Retrospection and anticipation were robbed of their sorrow and doubt, as the promises of God were mentioned
and the assurances of immortality remembered. To
each and all were the words of the Master welcome:

"Where I am, there shall also my servant be."

The heart of Siasconset throbs in sympathy with
Whitter's words, declaring

"That Life is ever lord of death,
And Love can never lose its own."

However impressively the night in its solemn stillness falls over the quiet village, the hours of day are far more numerous, in the time when the visitors add their life to its cottages, and so memory dwells most readily upon the early morning hours, the glow of noontide, and the sunset glory.

Hence, Helen possesses, embalmed in memory, a vivid picture of that morning brightness on the shore of the vast ocean, and she is not alone in declaring that among the most interesting sights in all the world, inspiring and uplifting, may be counted sunrise at Siasconset.

CHAPTER XI.

THE DEDICATION OF THE CHAPEL.

"In this communion sweet,
Hands clasp : hearts are replete
With joy—with pain ;
Our loved, with voices hushed,
Strengthen faith in the trust
'That, somewhere, meet we must,'
And live again."

ELIZABETH STARBUCK.

IMMORTALITY awaits us. So the average 'Scon-
seter believes, for he has perceived the "old, old
fashion of death," of which Charles Dickens speaks so
pathetically, and it is a comfort he would not forego to
receive also the idea of "that older fashion, Immortality." For almost a century, the rhymes called "'Sconset Laws," have familiarized their readers with the idea
that there is great, religious freedom in the sea-blest
village.

"Here invalids in Church and State
Are all made whole at 'Sconset."

But the time came when there was a large majority
who desired a summer chapel. A place of worship was
at last erected. Men and women of all grades of belief
contributed the money needed for that purpose, and it
was with a gladness of heart like that of ancient Israel,
that, at last, the villagers and their summer guests were
able to say, with the Psalmist : "I was glad when they
said unto me, Let us go into the house of the Lord."

The day was bright. It was Thursday, July 26, 1883.
Some of the choice spirits in the town of Nantucket
found their way over the flowery plains to the village
on "the bank." And 'Sconset was in all its glory.
Villagers and summer visitors alike, wended their way
to the little chapel on New Street. It was of unpreten-
tious architecture, though it had a small tower, from
which the sound of a Sabbath call to worship was to issue,
and plain and neat as it was, the one window of colored
glass was sufficient to give an aesthetic air to the sacred
edifice.

The exercises, as might be expected, were unpreten-
tious, and consisted of addresses, prayers, the reading
of the Scriptures, and sacred song, accompanied by the
music of a small, parlor organ. Addresses were made
by Rev. J. A. Savage, pastor of the Unitarian church in
Nantucket ; Rev. W. R. Eastman, Congregational pastor

in South Framingham, Mass.; and Rev. Phebe A.
Hanaford, at that time Universalist pastor in Jersey
City, N. J. Prayers were offered by Rev. J. Albert
Wilson, Unitarian pastor in Bridgewater, Mass.;* Rev.
P. D. Cowan, (Congregational) of Wellesley, Mass.; and
the benediction was given, finally, by Rev. L. Boyer,
the rector of St. Paul's Church, Nantucket. The Scriptures were admirably read by Rev. Louise S. Baker, the
beloved woman-pastor of the Congregational church in
Nantucket. There was then "variety in unity," at this
dedication of the Union chapel at 'Sconset.

Bright flowers adorned the pulpit, and the music was
so in keeping with the high character of the rare occasion that all hearts were wafted heavenward in sympathy with the tones that had in them more of heaven than
earth. Of those who sang, as well of those who spoke,
some have already passed to the world of light and
glory,

> " Where congregations ne'er break up,
> And Sabbaths have no end."

Only one of the addresses was written, and that was
by the woman whose island birth and training had given
her more opportunity than any other of the speakers, to

---

* Since deceased.

know the circumstances which made the matter of erect-
ing a place of worship at so late a period, so entirely
reasonable, though it appeared so strange unto the
summer visitors.

Rev. Mrs. Hanaford spoke from John iv., 23, 24, in
the following words:

DEDICATORY ADDRESS.

"Our blessed Master said to the astonished listener
who had always worshipped on Mount Gerizim, and who
believed that Jesus, being a Jew, would declare that in
Jerusalem alone might the devout soul draw near to
God, the words that ring in the chambers of my soul
to-day, as the thought which we should not overlook, as
we come together, in reverent gladness, to set apart this
edifice to the special service of Almighty God, in the
customary Sabbath exercises of instruction, exhortation,
prayer and praise. It has already been consecrated by
the free-will offerings of those who believe in the value
of religious teachings and influences. It has been dedicated in the thought and prayer of those who desired it,
and labored for it, long before the architect planned it,
or the corner stone was laid. Souls that have never seen
it, and hardly call to mind the ground whereon it stands,
have watched the island papers with an interest as de-

vout as it was affectionate, and as much in the way of consecration as any services we can hold to-day. Heart and hand have devoted this edifice to the Lord, in desire, in purpose, in execution, but to-day, as we come to the place where we rejoice together, and say: 'Come, sing unto the Lórd a new song,' for the greatly-needed place of worship is now erected, 'let us remember the words of the Lord Jesus, how He said:'

'The hour cometh and now is, when the true worshipper shall worship the Father in spirit and in truth, for the Father seeketh such to worship Him. God is a Spirit, and they that worship Him must worship Him in spirit and in truth.'

And I call attention to these words just now and here in order to assert that, while I have earnestly desired a church edifice in this village, and am grateful that our eyes are permitted to behold this consummation of devout desire and effort, I am just as certain that worshippers have dwelt in this village, and that the incense of true prayer has arisen to God, and the reverent waiting before God that He approves, has been the experience of many souls who have dwelt here, though, for all those long years, there has been no edifice specially set apart for public worship. To our knowledge, during the two centuries and a quarter in which this island has been

inhabited by English-speaking people, there has been no
house of worship, but they who came hither at intervals,
were men and women who believed in finding God
within, as well as, and perhaps rather than, without.
Quakerism, in its most devout form, existed on this island
for more than a century, and every Quaker carried his
church edifice about with him. He looked into his own
heart, not to write, as the poet directed, but to adore. He
listened to the voices around him—the voices of nature
and of man—but he obeyed the voice within—the voice
of God—of the in-dwelling Christ—the Word that could
evermore be made flesh as the obedient soul carried out
in daily life the behest of the King enthroned above the
human will. Hence, it was not that devout souls did
not visit this village, or tarry here, in the former days,
but that they really had not so much need—according
to their view of the matter—of a house of worship, and
so they did not build one, and their descendants copied
after them. That was one reason why no house of
prayer was ever erected here, and another was, that only
for a brief season, during any year, did families reside
here, and abundant provision was made for the needs of
worshippers in the good, old town, eight miles away.
When they were at home, they all had opportunities to
assemble themselves together for worship. When they

were away at 'Sconset, or anywhere, beside, upon the face
of the globe—the Quakers among them, at least, could
worship, alone or together, indoors or out, and be content.

It is almost within my memory that families have
resided here the year round.   This also will account for
the fact that no church had been erected here till now.
But the need came with the increasing population, and
with the fact that children were in households whose
stay was continuous.   When the vibration of families
between 'Sconset and Nantucket ceased, and the winter
hours as well as summer ones were to be spent here by
families, it was perceived that a place for religious services was needed, and, as in many small communities,
the school-house was used for a church, as opportunity
for religious instruction and worship was afforded.
Visiting ministers from Nantucket, visiting ministers
from abroad (notably the sainted Lucretia Mott) lifted
their voices with the word of power and blessing in that
little school-house, till it has become to many souls a place
of inspiring and hallowed association.*   But in the
Providence that is in unslumbering—the inevitable and
beneficent working of divine law—this village has become a place of rest and needed recreation to a far larger
number of men, women and children, than the early

---

* There the speaker preached her first sermon, in 1865.

8

visitors could ever have dreamed would sojourn here,
and then came the necessity for a more commodious
place of worship. The divine law of demand and sup-
ply—the fulfillment of His purpose who marketh all our
necessities—has sent hither those who felt the need of the
time, and had the means to assist in meeting it. Christian zeal and enthusiasm, friendly interest and benevo-
lent purpose, have done the work, under the guiding
Providence of God, that has brought us to this hour of
victory and rejoicing. One after another the obstacles
have been met, and, by kind hearts and willing hands,
been conquered; till to-day this little church lifts its
spire heavenward, and tells to every visitor, who rises over
yonder, grassy hill-top, from the flowery plain beyond,
that He who stretched the blue and sparkling waters
before them, and is saying to the ocean when its billows
rise amid the storms that sometimes howl around us,—
'thus far shalt thou come, and no farther, and there
shall thy proud waves be stayed,'—He is recognized,
and, Sabbath after Sabbath, worshipped with the voice
of prayer and praise. Worship was here before the
island Indians built their wigwams, for the ocean waves
lifted their solemn voices before the history of our race
began. And still they worship, and we feel their inspiration.

' The ocean looketh up to heaven,
    As 'twere a living thing,
The homage of its waves is given
    In ceaseless worshipping.

They kneel upon the sloping sands
    As bends the human knee—
A beautiful, a tireless band—
    The priesthood of the sea.'

The Indian was God's child. He was not undevout. He was of those who could see God in the sunset clouds we watch with reverent interest, and hear Him in the mighty storm-wind which bids us lift the cry, 'God save the mariner upon the dangerous coast !' Worship was here, the Indian bowing before the Great Spirit, and looking forward, with all the light he had, to better days upon the happy hunting-ground. And when the greater Light came with the race which is in every land showing the divine law of ' the survival of the fittest,' surely there was worship then. He worships God who helps his fellow man. The Baptist, Peter Folger,* the Quaker, Mary (Coffin) Starbuck,† worshipped, and not alone ! Among their descendants, and the descendants of those who were with them in those far-off years have

* Maternal grandfather of Benjamin Franklin.
† The "great Mary Starbuck" daughter of Tristram Coffin.

ever been found true worshippers who have—with
forms or without forms—with outward or with inward
reverence—or both—respected Gospel truth, and adored
the 'One God, and Father of all, who is above all,
through all, and in you all.'

The procession of the years and the generations have
brought us here to continue the voice of worship which
Nature and Humanity so long ago began. Let us, as
we now dedicate this welcome edifice, so long desired, re-
dedicate our own hearts also to the worship of Almighty
God, our ever-loving Father and eternal Friend, endeav-
oring so to live each secular day of our earthly lives, as
well as every Sabbath day—that we shall help to carry
out the evident design of Jesus when he said the true
worshipper shall 'worship the Father in spirit and in
truth, for the Father seeketh such to worship Him.
God is a spirit, and they that worship Him must worship Him in spirit and in truth.' As John Weiss wrote,
so let us say—

> ' The truest worship is a life—
>   All dreaming I resign ;
>   We lay our offering at thy feet ;
>   Our lives, O Christ, are Thine !' "

Thus ended the address of the woman-preacher on
that day. And so, with loving thought of many who

had dwelt in 'Sconset cottages, and from those lowly homes had gone to the many mansions of the Father's house, the speaker and others "thanked God and took courage," for the little chapel stood for faith, and hope, and love,—it meant God here and everywhere,—and it stood also for a belief in Immortality.

CHAPTER XII.

THE NEPHEWS.

" Hast thou ofttimes our island been on,
    To seek for food to break thy fast ?
And did'st thou think that thy broad pinion
    Had brought thee here to breath thy last ?"

ELIZA BARNEY.

THUS sang one of the cultured, island women—a descendant of "the great Mary Starbuck!" that renowned daughter of Tristram Coffin, who was one of the judges in the land, when the dwellers on Nantucket were but few, and the Indians still lingered in their native haunts.   The lines are a part of a soliloquy over an owl which had been shot by a sportsman, and might often be said of other owls prepared by the taxidermist for those visitors who adorn their libraries with the bird of wisdom. Owls may be found on Nantucket, natives as well as visitors, and their hoot is often heard on the road over the moor to 'Sconset, as well as round Tom Nevers pond, which seems to be a favorite resort.   They are usually small and brown.   It is said that while little local interest is as yet displayed in regard to ornithology, still "Nantucket furnishes a rare field for the study of migratory birds, it being the last place they leave after their season in the regular breeding places farther up the coast. From Nantucket, they pass to the capes below into warmer weather." Thus the island is a resort for the sportsman as well as others, and the gun, as well as the fish-line, is considered part of the complete equipment of a young man who is a 'Sconset visitor. Tradition states that a well-known lady-poet of the island, for many years a teacher, once narrowly escaped being shot, as, in her season of rambling, after the school at 'Sconset was closed, she sat behind a sort of sand-dune on the beach, her head, or hat, being mistaken for a good sized bird in the distance. As the gunner approached so as to get a fair shot, the head moved, the bird-like appearance was gone, and Miss Anna Gardner was spared to add yet further to her labors for humanity, and to the well-deserved honors which greet her declining years.

The N. M. had told this story of a narrow escape for a score of times or more (her long-cherished fear of a gun having stamped it in memory) when Rollie—the Boston nephew—came running into the "Auntie" who was always ready to meet emergencies, and displayed a finger which had been injured while using a small pistol, and the ever-ready and willing Helen soon had it in charge.

"You ought to have been a physician and surgeon!" said Rollie, when the finger was duly dressed and made comfortable, and all the hearers said "Amen," each after his and her own fashion. Helen did possess natural aptitude for rendering medical or surgical aid, in such cases, and was often in demand. Day after day Rollie came, with his wounded finger, poisoned also by the explosive substance used, and received the wise and patient attention of the helpful Helen, which alone prevented serious results. At last Rollie could play lawn-tennis once more, and then the evidence that he was a pet of his late doctor was observed when it was perceived that he was not allowed to bemoan the fact that his lawn-tennis suit had been soiled, and there was no one handy to cleanse it. Amid the smiles of those beholding how he could govern Helen, who never saw anything amiss in his boyish capers, the long hose and white doublet soon appeared in a spotless condition, and Rollie was himself again. The boy-visitors at 'Sconset are often "in clover." And for that matter, so are the girl-visitors, for they bathe and swim, talk and walk, play tennis, and wait at the post-office together. 'Sconset vacation joys make halcyon days for memory to garner. And health and happiness, with fresh air and good food, and pleasant companionship, are the portion of the youth who are favored to spend the summer weeks where neighborly good-will abounds and 'Sconset laws are obeyed.

One night there was a rush in the little cottage. Two boys rushed in—Two Waltham boys—the dear nephews of the sister-aunties. What a happy greeting! One boy could be called a man; in size and spirit he was a man, and the School of Technology in Boston never had a more worthy student. The other, a boy of fourteen, was stout as a farmer's son might be who did not fail to do his fair share of farm work: and intelligent as a High School boy of great promise must necessarily be. He was another " Rollie "—named for the same dear 'Sconset boy who went in the footsteps of his whalemen ancestors, and alas! returned no more.

Capt. Baxter, the renowned Munchausen of 'Sconset— had brought the boys in his " side-wheel craft" safely, beguiling the tedium of the slow ride in the sea-fog, with his many tales, more or less colored and discolored. Evincing remarkable activity for one of his years—fourscore and more—the venerable captain has won many friends, having a kind heart despite his rough-and-ready

speech, and proving a true friend to many in their times
of need.

On the next day after their arrival, word came that
the surf was very high, and there was a rush for the
beach. What mighty waves! How they rolled in, and
up around the tent poles and the hammocks! Chairs
were hastily carried farther up the beach:—every movable thing was put out of reach of the invading breakers, whose loud roar was appalling to those unused to
such watery strife.

Afterwards, in recalling the scene, all agreed that
Northrop had most vividly depicted their experience
that day in his words:—"you see a wave of unusual mag-
nitude rolling in from far beyond the wild revelry of
waters on 'the rips.' It leaps into the arena, as if fresh
and eager for the prey, clutches another Bacchanal like
itself, and the two towering floods rush swiftly toward
the shore. Instinctively you run backward to escape
what seems an impending destruction. Very likely a
sheet of foam is dashed all around you, shoe-deep, but
you are safe—only the foam hisses at you in impotent
rage. The sea has its bounds: 'hitherto shalt thou come,
but no farther.' Mighty and terrible within its own
domain, and beating wildly upon the shore, century
after century, it yet obeys the law which is mightier

than it, and abides within its own limits—powerful to
destroy, yet obedient to the last."

It was a grand, yet fearful, sight, to behold those
mighty breakers gather strength, as it seemed, rise in a
lofty crest, and, bending in a lordly way, pour forth
their waters as they dashed upon the shore. Over and
over again. There was a fascination in the sight.
Each wave was watched to see if it was the superior or
inferior of the one which preceded it. And the roar of
the tumultous breakers was itself exciting. One seemed
a part of the commotion. Wave against wave far out
beyond the breakers, tossing their white crests proudly
and defiantly, and at our feet the gathered forces smit-
ing the sandy beach with a roar that drowned the human
voice, and a solemn asseveration of power that awed and
hushed the beholder.

The shadows of evening were gathering, before the
nephews, and those who enjoyed their enthusiasm and
shared it, left the beach. And afterward, whenever
they talked of it, and of the waves as they appeared
next day, all over the wide expanse reaching from 'Sconset Bank to the "Old Man"—a white-capped shoal far
off on the Eastern horizon—their sentiments were seen
to be identical with Mr. Northrop's, when he said*—

---

* "'Sconset Cottage Life." p. 144.

"I think I never saw anything in all my life that impressed me as did this battle of waves and tide on 'the rips'—not even Niagara. There you comprehend the cause—the fall of water—gravitation. Here it is the mystery of the tide, the dominion of the moon contending with the waves that themselves—the wind meanwhile having already ceased—seem as mysterious. Here is an upheaval, a wild, tumultous conflict of waters that ought, to all appearances to be as calm and peaceful as a lakelet. There seems, indeed, to be life, will,—and a malignant will,—anger and ferocity, in this desperate struggle, that are demoniac. And it is perhaps this element of the wonderful exhibition of Nature's forces that makes the scene peculiarly impressive."

  Never, in after life, can those who are reared on the sea-shore forget the impression of wild and stormy grandeur which the surf presents during an on-shore gale, or after a storm at sea.

CHAPTER XIII.

SEA-STORIES.

"I know an isle, clasped in the sea's strong arms,
　　Sport of his rage, and sharer of his dreams;
　　A barren spot to alien eyes it seems,
　　But for its own it wears unfailing charms."

　　　　　　　　　　EMILY SHAW FORMAN.

O listen to those talkers out there! Their speaking is what you may call *animated!*" exclaimed Helen, and those to whom she spoke looked out of the side window, and saw the aged sea-captain, and some younger men sitting on the little bench by the store, and their faces as well as voices expressed deep interest in the conversation.

"They are telling stories of whaling days, I guess," said the N. M.

"Telling yarns," laughingly responded Helen, "and they are like parrots, all talkers but no hearers."

"Wait a few minutes," said the invalid. "They will settle down, and you will find that Capt. George

W. Coffin will have the floor. I have observed that his voice out-sounds the rest in the long run, and they like to hear his well-told sea-tales too well not to be silent after awhile."

"His oft-told," said the N. M., "for he has told them for a half-century or more."

"The same ones?" queried Helen, "and without embellishment?"

"Yes, the same, and without parallax. He steers a straight course always!" and the N. M. paused with an expression which said, "Don't you doubt my father's sea-stories, if you do those of every other story-teller!"

Helen and the invalid smiled, and responded to the look with a nod of approval. And then they listened.

The ancient mariner was telling a modern tale whose items had all been rehearsed in the ears of the family and visitors many times. It concerned himself as the keeper of the Life-Boat. *The* Life-Boat, *par excellence*, for when he first took charge of it there was no Life-Saving Service established on the island, or indeed on the coast of the United States anywhere. A few such boats as the one he cared for, and a few huts known as "Humane houses," because belonging to the Massachusetts Humane Society, were all the evidences afforded, to show that those safe on land were interested to rescue the imperilled toilers of the sea.

The old captain prided himself on taking good care of the boat, and regarded himself as sole custodian of the property which was in his hands. No coaxing could get the keys. If any one wished to see the boat he would go to the boat-house with him. Otherwise no vision. One Sunday morning, a well dressed gentleman came, and desired to see the boat, saying, "Let me have the keys, and I will soon return them." But the sturdy old custodian refused. The visitor urged. It was all in vain. Evidently he thought the old captain was uncivil and disobliging. Baffled and annoyed, the visitor asked why he was so persistent, and indicated that he might at least allow *him* to have the keys. The captain looked out of the door, and saw the elegant carriage and two horses, but he was not awed by equipage or apparel, and finally declared that as there was no wreck, and it was the Sabbath, he was not bound even to show anybody the way to the boat, and he had kept those keys for twenty years or more, and proposed to hold on to them. It was with him duty and conscience, and he wouldn't budge an inch.

"But," said he, when he had given full evidence of his faithful stewardship in the particular of keeping the keys, like a veritable Protestant Saint Peter, "I will go with you, and open the boat-house door myself."

And he enjoyed the change of look that came to his visitor, with a quiet smile. But no persuasion could induce him to ride. He trudged along, after his usual manner, the carriage slowly following, and when the boat had been examined, was surprised to find that this visitor was an official of the Humane Society who had heard of Capt. Coffin's indomitable persistency in keeping the keys, and had that day seen that they could not be obtained by any show of wealth or station, but all favors consistent with his duty would be courteously granted. So the official praised his trustworthiness, and thereafter the faithful custodian delighted to tell the simple story, in his own graphic language, over and over again. And that tale he was shouting forth to his hearers that morning, with all the accompaniments of gesticulation needful, and the " He said," and " says I," that help to make narration impressive.

As the story came to its climax and close, to the evident satisfaction of speaker and listeners, the invalid sagely remarked—" How much of the interest of a story, and of conversation generally, depends upon the picturing of the scene by those little words " He said," and " says I!"

" Even so, my sapient sister !" exclaimed Helen, " a narrative and a recital are always essentially different."

"Well, I must confess I am interested as much in the manner of telling a story as I am in the story itself."

"So are my father's hearers," responded the N. M., "for it is his emphatic use of hands and arms, and voice, that makes them patiently listen to-day to the unimportant stories he is telling. But he has some veritable sea-stories worth telling, and you ought to hear them."

Helen laughed aloud, and exclaimed, "Do you remember the time we were going to be quiet in your study, and you gave your father some pictures to keep him still and happy, as he rested on the lounge, and you were calmly writing at your study-table?"

"Indeed I do," answered the N. M., "and how he almost fancied the lounge a whale-boat, and like some old soldier 'fighting his battles o'er again,' he appeared to tackle the leviathan, and every picture only increased his ardor, and the force and compass of his voice, and the vigor of motion in arms and tongue, till we gave up the pen and were his audience from the time the whale was sighted, with 'There she blows!' till the trying out of the oil began."

"Why, what caused the commotion?" wonderingly asked the invalid.

"We had handed him a series of engravings repre-

9

senting the capture of a whale. It proved anything but
a sedative for him or us," quickly responded Helen, and
she and the N. M. laughed heartily over the well-remembered episode.

A little time after this conversation the captain had
opportunity to tell a genuine whale-story, and the invalid had a specimen of what was seen and heard that
night in the unquiet study, and very much wished she
could reproduce it in his own language for her pupils
and friends in coming days.

Very tamely it is here re-produced. He said that he
was in a boat, rowing after a whale. He was boat-steerer,
and the mate was in the bow of the boat. The whale
had been struck, and the line had a turn round the log-
gerhead and was "nippered," while the whale was running on the top of the water. The occupants of the boat
thought all the whales of that school were ahead, keeping together like a herd of cows, when lo ! a huge whale
rose right under them. The concussion sent the boat-
steerer, and a youngster, who was aft next the steering
oar, some forty or fifty feet into the air, and as the two
boats were running nearly side by side, they landed in
the other boat, safe from further harm ; four of the
boat's crew were left in the water, the mate reached for
his knife and cut off the line which was fast to the

whale, and then the rest held on to their boat till the captain came with his boat, and took them in, and towed the broken boat back to the ship, which was then about a mile to the leeward. Meanwhile the whales had disappeared.

The tameness of this narration gives but a feeble glimpse of the excitement of such an hour of daring and of danger. But to hear these tales of the whalers from those who were eye-witnesses, and partakers of the heroism and peril, is worth a journey to Nantucket. Only a little while, and the last of the old sea-captains, who followed the ocean monster to his haunts, will be "gathered to his fathers," and there will be no more such wonderful narrations, or such graphic narrators, for the whale and the whaler will both be things of the past.

"Do you wonder," asked the N. M., "that when I was a child I used to sit upon my father's knee, and recite to him the twenty-three stanzas—ninety-two lines —written by Peleg Folger, in which the whale was mentioned?"

"I am not surprised," laughingly answered Helen, "Not a hair rises in amazement."

"Perhaps you will be amused, if not amazed, if I should give you a few stanzas. Listen!"

"Thou dids't, O Lord, create the mighty whale,
    That wondrous monster of a mighty length ;
Vast is the head and body, vast his tail,
    Beyond conception his immeasured strength.

When he the surface of the sea hath broke,
    Arising from the dark abyss below,
His breath appears a lofty stream of smoke,
    The circling waves like glittering banks of snow.

But, everlasting God, thou dost ordain,
    That we, poor feeble mortals should engage
(Ourselves, our wives, and children to maintain)
    This dreadful monster with a martial rage.

And though he furiously doth us assail,
    Thou dost preserve us from all dangers free ;
He cuts our boat in pieces with his tail,
    And spills us all at once into the sea."

As the N. M. paused, Helen suggested that the other
nineteen stanzas could be dispensed with, and the N. M.
assented with the words: "That's enough.   The author
died when my grandmother was seven years old, and I
suppose two generations had recited them in their childhood, if not three, before I got hold of them.   They
are a part of Nantucket's classics."

"So are Mrs. Forman's 'sonnets,'" said Helen, "and
a decided improvement."

"Perhaps in accordance with the law of evolution," added the invalid, and the conversation closed, for it was bathing time. The white umbrella with its green lining, was taken out to become "the tent on the beach," and with a sense of exhilaration in the very thought of the sounding sea, and the sandy beach, and the pleasant fellowship, the trio left the cottage, and hastened down the bank.

CHAPTER XIV.

DANGER OFF 'SCONSET.

"But 'Sconset saw a cruel sight:
　The mocking rage of the ' Old Man's ' might;
　Stood and beheld within their reach,
　Beyond the surf of the long, Low Beach,
　A sinking vessel—' God pity the men !'
　The terrible shoal devouring them then.
　And many a craft with a tattered sail,
　Went down in the merciless wave and gale ;
　And many a man was lost that night,
　With never a star when the sea grew white!"

　　　　　　　ARTHUR ELWELL JENKS.

"HERE'S your spy glass, grandfather!" exclaimed
Rollie, one morning, just-after breakfast, as he
rushed in from the bank, where he and the other boys
had been watching the mighty billows as they rolled
along, breaking in snowy foam long before they reached
the sandy beach.

The old sea-captain turned hastily around, the fire
came to his eyes, but instead of telling the wide-awake
grandson where the coveted spy-glass was placed, he

asked: "What is there to see? is there a wreck?" For the earnest manner of the active boy betokened something more than usual, and the spy-glass was not to be relinquished to one of the third generation while the old Commissioner of wrecks was able to look after things himself.

The boy had to answer that a fishing smack was amid the wild waters bearing down upon Pochick Rip, and the men, on the bank watching her, were alarmed for her safety.

The old veteran of the seas had been bemoaning his inability to walk far on account of lameness, but "as a man thinketh, so is he," and as he jumped for his pea-jacket and sou-wester, and took the glass under his arm, no one would have thought his feet were weary, or that his limbs were heavy with the weight of four score years. Out he went, into the rain and mist and wild blasts of that August gale—"What was a north-east storm to him if a vessel was in peril?"

The female portion of the household were a little longer in putting on rubbers and waterproofs, etc., and when they reached the street, "grandpa" was out of sight. And actually!—such was the force of mind over matter on such an occasion that before they could reach "the gully" they could see "Father Coffin" returning

with the assurance of safety, given in a stentorian voice,
" All ship-shape! They've run under the lea at Tom
Nevers!" and, long afterward, was that disturbed household, that sudden departure with the hugged-up spy-
glass, that rapid apparelling of the women folks, that
hasty return of the sea-king with a shout of victory,
mentioned as evidence that the changing of thought
gave strength to weakness, and lent wings to feet apparently too lame to walk.   No getting cold at such times!
No hesitancy through fear, and therefore no physical
results such as fearful hesitancy in the path of duty may
always be expected to bring.

When all was over, and the women also had returned,
there were questionings and answers concerning ship-
wrecks off 'Sconset, and as the stories of danger and
distress were told rapidly, one after the other, by the
old sea-captain and some of the neighbors who had
dropped in, when the flurry which stirred the heart of
Siasconset was all over, and the imperilled craft was
anchored safely under the lea, the N. M. declared it
was not strange that years ago an island poet had
pictured the rugged pathway of the mariners off 'Sconset in a storm, in the words, speaking of the sea-girt
island:

"Thy fatal shores, and sandy shoals,
   Round which the foaming white-cap rolls,
      All hopes of safety blast ;
   The pale, affrighted sailor eyes
   The dangers that around him rise,
      And turns away aghast."

"I can remember," said the N. M., "when the beach
was much narrower than it is now, for I came up here
to 'Sconset for a fishing season with my grand-parents,
when I was a girl, and we occupied a little cottage in
the front row ; and that row is all gone now ; washed
away, the bank is, and the houses taken to pieces and
moved away, where they were not undermined so they
fell. The beach was so short, the waves touched the
bank, even when the sea was not in a rage. I was a little school-girl—about ten years old—why its almost fifty
years ago !—and as our goods had not arrived, for heavy
loads over heavy sands move slowly, I betook me to the
only book I could find in the cottage, and I remember
that I sat on the table, with my feet in a chair, so that
I might see the surf as it rose and broke and rolled up
toward the foot of the hill, and read, when I was not
watching the waves, and the sea-gulls and the foamy
surf.

"And what did you read ? Can you remember that?"
asked the invalid.

"Indeed I can remember the small, quarto, leather-covered volume."

"And it was—

"Walker's Dictionary." All burst into a laugh at the mental picture of a little girl reading the dictionary, because there was nothing else to read.

"Just like you!" said Helen with a twinkle in her eye which suggested raillery—"I wonder you didn't write verses, as well as read the dictionary."

"Perhaps I should, if I had been equipped with pencil and paper," was the answer, with a quiet smile. "I signed a receipt once with a nail dipped in ink, when at moving-time the household goods had gone, leaving only the ink-bottle on the mantel. But that was in after years," she added with a sigh, "when I was about to remove from my island home."

"How vivid the remembrances of childhood are!" said the invalid, musingly. "I think I could never forget the storms around Nantucket, if I had seen them with childish eyes, and grieved over them with childhood's heart of timid sympathy!"

"You may be sure children do remember such things," responded the N. M., "for I well remember how I stood up in a chair, and watched a little vessel coming across the rips in a heavy sea, and how my dear, good

stepmother cried and sobbed as she stood near me, and
held her breath, at times, as the vessel rose and fell and
was sometimes almost out of sight. She had known
what it was to have a brother go to sea in a vessel like
that, and after one of these storms, another vessel
reached the island, and reported the foundering of her
brother's craft with all on board. It had been seen
laboring amid the surges, and then it sank into the
trough of the sea and was lost to view forever. It had
sunk to rise no more. Her brother Rowland never
reached his home again."

"These narrations make a sea-faring life seem unat-
tractive to me," said the invalid.

"But," said Helen, "I suppose there are those to
whom the daring and the danger would really have a
charm, or there would be no whalers, no explorers, and
commerce would cease between ocean-divided lands."

"We have evidence of that in the past history of this
island. Its name has become almost synonymous with
bravery in the midst of ocean's perils, and I do believe
the old whalers really felt 'at home on the rolling deep,'"
was the last word on the subject, spoken by the N. M.,
who lost no opportunity of sounding the praises of her
native island, and its brave and hardy sons and self-
reliant daughters.

CHAPTER XV.

SYMPATHY.

" Over the road to 'Sconset,
    That dear, old sea-blown place,
The dreamy fisher-hamlet,
    Where smiles the ocean's face ;
Over the road to 'Scorset
    I'm riding all alone ;
And the sunset's sweet reflections;
    Are warmly akin to my own."

ANNA C. STARBUCK.

THE surf was still high, and ran far up the sandy beach. All night long, its continuous roar had been heard by those who were not lost in slumber, and its monotone mingled with the dreams of those who slept. But, before morning, the roar was louder, for the wind which had lulled, had again arisen, the tide also had attained its majority, so to speak, and every wave seemed a tenth, each was so full and strong and rolled up on the beach so far. It was a grand morning for those who wished to see the ocean in a tumult.

Not now in a rage. Not in a fury yet, as when in winter storms, or mad, October gales, the whole wide expanse was white-capped, turbulent strife, but enough in a commotion to satisfy those who knew little of the phases which old ocean can put on, and who are ready to watch the ceaseless heavings with alternate wonder and awe, mingled at times with a sort of wild delight.

But the sun was peering through the clouds, and they were rolling away. The village was in ecstasies.

The little folks were confident the wind would go down soon, and even if the surf did not subside, so that they could bathe, at least the children could enjoy being on the beach again. And as for the children of a larger growth, they were just as glad to see the sun as the younger people were.

"To see the sun is pleasant," now as in Bible times, and despite the lack of shade trees, 'Sconset folks and their visitors all welcome the sun, trusting to umbrellas and to large hats for escape from browning, and really not caring a copper if they do get "as brown as a berry."

On such a morning as this, George stopped under the window, and called aloud to the people within. "Halloo there! want a ride? Halloo! come out and ride!"

The invitation was soon accepted. No stylish equipage awaited the party, and no affectation of style pre-

vented the ladies from mounting into the wagon, and
riding off up to the vegetable garden. It was "out
North," George said, and it was worth seeing when it was
reached. Such nice beans, and squashes, and green corn!
And, on the way, how many wild flowers! It was a rich
treat after the storm; and the two sisters did so enjoy
the flora of the island!*   And then the ride itself! No
formality of dress! No repression of speech or laugh!
It was 'Sconset, and the heart of Siasconset was sympathetic with all the phases of feeling which move to smiles
or tears: so if one chose to laugh aloud, or sing, or shout
merrily, or talk like parrots, there was no infringement
of etiquette, and Mrs. Grundy did not elevate her tip-
tilted nose and say : "Such people!"

In summer time 'Sconset was hardly to be called a
"dreamy fisher-hamlet," for there was little opportunity
for dreams, except in the night, or just after dinner. All
the same it is a "dear old, sea-blown place," and the
fresh, morning air was exhilarating as the visitors to
Coffyn Cottage rode up to "the lot," and rode back
with the vegetables. That was a ride to be held in
memory. That was a morning of joyous sympathies.

---

* Since that memorable summer, a valuable Catalogue of the Plants of Nantucket has been published, prepared by Mrs. Maria L. Owen, of Springfield, Mass.,
a native of Nantucket, and a descendant of its most honored early settlers. It is
extensive and accurate, and invaluable to all who love, or would learn about, the
flora of Nantucket.

But not all the mornings were care-free. There was much to be done to make life comfortable. Even in cottages there are beds to make, lamps to trim, dishes to cleanse, and various other domestic duties, attention to which is not to be avoided, and which take time and strength. And one morning there came which was full of sorrowful sympathy.

A brother's wife came in with a sad face. Tears gathered in her eyes. All saw that something had occurred to make the motherly heart very heavy.

"Why, Mary Eliza!" exclaimed Helen, "you look troubled! What's the matter? Anybody sick, at your house?"

"Nobody is sick," was the reply, as the kind-hearted visitor sank wearily into a chair, "but that dear, little baby is dead." And then the tears, which had been welling up from the heart of one who had not forgotten her own blessed infant, long ago gone into the angels' keeping, gathered in the blue eyes and slowly rolled down her cheeks, as she sobbed out, "I kept the baby's milk by itself, and we have been careful it should have the very best, and when they came up this morning, they said it was no longer needed, for the dear, little baby was dead."

The heart of Siasconset had been full of sympathy in

reference to that sweet babe, which was struggling for
life, during the teething period, and would have been
victor on 'Sconset bank, if anywhere on earth; but its
days were numbered, and after watching and waiting,
and as it were the very holding of breath in the village
to listen to the plaintive wailing of the feeble infant, the
time had come when the mother was to find her arms
empty, and the whole of the little community was to
be saddened in sympathy with her maternal grief.

"I wanted to send some flowers," continued the kind,
motherly sympathiser, "but I had none save large and
gay ones. They didn't seem appropriate for that sweet,
little babe."

"Oh!" said Helen, always equal to every emergency,
"you forgot the lovely, white, wild flowers around us.
I'll make you a wreath, if you'll get me some of them."

And sure enough! only a little while, and on a large
plate, holding water to keep it fresh, lay a lovely, white
and green wreath, prepared by Helen's deft fingers and
consummate taste, and Mary Eliza carried the simple
offering to the little cottage in White's Hamlet, and
left it as a token of the fact that the farmer's wives not
only sell milk to their summer customers, but that the
hearts of Siasconset people are touched in tender sympathy with all the woes and griefs which may come to

the fellow beings—their brothers and sisters of the Continent—who seek health and recreation on their shores.
From the hour when the sweet baby ceased to suffer,
the heart of Siasconset throbbed in sympathy with the
bereaved. As previously stated, the old fashion of
death, which Dickens mentioned, when Paul Dombey's
soul went out with the tide, has long been known in that
sea-side village. Thank God, it has also known of that
"older fashion—immortality!"

And Helen softly whispered to the N. M. that night,
referring to the dear baby-angel, and quoting a poem
published in her own compilation,* and written by a
friend of her girlhood:

> "High in those eternal archways
>   By the white celestials trod,
> Baby's learned the hidden password
>   Of the mystic lodge of God."

The precious dust of the little infant was, next morning, borne far away to Detroit, and the heart of Siasconset followed the bereaved parents, on their sorrowful
way, with tender sympathy, with prayers and tears.

---

* "Our Home Beyond The Tide," page 226.

CHAPTER XVI.

"THE GREAT MARY STARBUCK."

"God bless the sea-beat island,
    And grant forevermore,
That charity and freedom dwell
    As now, upon her shore!"

                              JOHN G. WHITTIER.

EVER since the days of which the Quaker poet sang in his poem of "The Exiles" there has been an atmosphere of freedom and good will upon the island to which Thomas Macy and Edward Starbuck betook themselves, when persecuted for harboring Quakers. And the island, in later years, became the dwelling place of scores of Quakers—nay hundreds, who by "convincement," or "birthright," belonged to the peaceful sect. The N. M. seemed to enjoy speaking of this fact, and prided herself on her Quaker ancestry. And she appeared rather to be pleased when she set up patriotism against Quakerism, as she recounted to her patient hearers, again and again, the time when she rose up in a Baptist prayer-meeting in a busy shore-town of Massachusetts—

after some of the best blood of Essex County had been shed for liberty—and declared in rhymes of her own arranging:

> " Child of the peaceful sect though I was born,
> Taught the brave warrior and his deeds to scorn,
> Yet, if I must, my birthright I resign,
> And henceforth own my country's cause is mine!"

But, after all, how the N. M. did love to see the simple, but attractive Quaker garb! How she did like to go over to "Cousin Sarah's" and listen to her cheerful "thee" and "thou," and when "Cousin George" saw fit to hold forth in the school-house, or the hotel parlor, she had gone many a time, not so much to hear him deliver his message, it is true, as to live over again the days of old, when, in the town eight miles away, she had spent many a Sabbath of her childhood listening to the anthem music of Mary (Clisby) Macy, (whose ninety-second year found her still on the island full of faith and hope), and where on rare occasions the Gospel melody of Sybil Jones* was heard, and the impressible heart of girlhood was stirred to lofty emotion and consecrated purposes!

So when "Hepsibeth" came, with her "companion,"

---

* A renowned Quaker preacher mentioned in Harriet Beecher Stowe's "Sunny Memories of Foreign Lands."

and other friends, it was with no small delight that the
N. M. and many others of the 'Sconset households sat
willingly in the waiting silence, and then listened with
satisfaction to the words of peace. Even during the
week-day hours there were some who felt willing to turn
aside for a season of prayer and praise, and solemn communion with each other and with God.

The N. M. was a reverent believer in the call of
women to be helpful in the world, as preachers, if they
pleased, and in all other ways, and she was never weary
of singing the praises of those Nantucket women who
in their day and generation had exerted wide influence
as preachers or reformers. She did not forget the names
of Lucretia Mott, and Eliza Barney, but she went back
often to the name of Mary Starbuck, the grandmother,
several generations back, of Eliza Barney, and the ancestral relative also of Lucretia Mott:—Lucretia, having
been born "Coffin," and Mary Starbuck being Mary
Coffin, the daughter of the first chief magistrate, Tristram Coffin. She enjoyed therefore the perusal of a
book published in 1833 and entitled "Female Biog-
raphy." On its 463 page was the following sketch of
the renowned Mary Starbuck, who was a Quaker preacher,
and a sort of Deborah, upon the island, in her day. The
author, Samuel L. Knapp, says:

" MARY STARBUCK. If we look at the origin of every
country, state, or colony, we shall find that the women
had more to do with the foundation of their prosperity
than the men; but it has so happened, I will not say by
design, but rather by the course of events, that but few
of them have been fairly placed on the pages of history. There is a small island within the limits of Mas-
sachusets, known to most of the world from the enter-
prise and wealth of its inhabitants, whose history is
unique—this is the island of Nantucket. In 1659, it
was taken possession of by two white men and their
families, Thomas Macy and Edward Starbuck. They
fled, when the Quakers were persecuted, and settled on
this island. They were joined by others who were apprehensive of being involved with Hugh Peters, a
preacher of note, who had been prominent in the revo-
lution which brought Charles I. to the scaffold. On
the restoration of his son, Charles II., the whole world
was searched for those who had been unfriendly to his
father. Among these, perhaps, although not of great
importance, were those who settled in Nantucket, for
while they lived at Salisbury on the Merrimack, they
had been intimate friends of Hugh Peters. People in a
primitive state always discriminate more accurately than
those of a more advanced standing. The aborigines sel-

dom have a coward for their leader. Mary Starbuck, the wife of one of those first settlers of Nantucket, was a woman of superior mind. The influence of that mind commenced when she had but few or no rivals; and for more than half a century, she exercised that control, which great sagacity and sound sense, with virtuous principles, always deserve to have. This people saw their insular situation, and knew that as they increased, the soil could not be depended upon, alone, for subsistence, and they made their harvests on the waves of the ocean, a territory which no agrarian law could reach. Whales were seen dashing near them, and the sight was too tempting for them to refrain from the fishery. They knew nothing of the manner of harpooning them at that time, but by the advice of Mary Starbuck, they sent to Cape Cod for some persons acquainted with the business of catching whales. Interest is always quicksighted. By the advice of Mary Starbuck, the system which has characterized the whalers of Nantucket from all other co-partners, was established. 'Let each have an interest, and everyone will do his duty,' was her maxim.

More than sixty large ships are now owned in Nantucket, engaged in the whale fishery. The first whaling vessels were small; they went north, then south, and

in process of time swept round Cape Horn, when
larger vessels were built; and then they circumnavigated
the globe, in the course of their business. These whalers, perhaps, now little think how much they are in-
debted to Mary Starbuck for the first great principles
which now govern these voyages; and but little did Mary
Starbuck know of the oceans they were to explore; but
such is the power of mind, well directed in the early
stages of society. A curious subject of contemplation
naturally presents itself, as we see the proud whaling
ships, returning from their long voyages, laden with
valuable cargoes, and then run back to the origin and
progress of this great business, to the time when Mary
Starbuck saw her children and kindred set sail for the
monsters of the deep, in small boats, and return with
success.

If, at Nantucket, you inquire of the first one you meet
(and those islanders are an intelligent people) for the
monument raised to Mary Starbuck, the answer will be,
'Mary has no monument.' If you ask, 'Well then,
where was she buried?' 'Why, I never heard where;
but probably on that rising ground, as it is generally
understood that it was once used as a burial place, and
there is one small grave-stone there which goes to support the tradition.' If Mary Starbuck ever had a monu-

ment, the sands have blown over it, and it cannot be found at this day. Tradition does not assist us to speak precisely of the time of her death, but represents her as living to a good old age."

The N. M., closing the reading, thereupon remarked, that, as Mary Starbuck was a Quaker it is nearly certain that she had no stone at her grave, since Quakers were unwilling so far to conform to worldly customs as to have any sort of a stone, until within the last half century, so that the N. M. cannot even find the place where her own mother rests.

The whaling fleet has all departed; the lucrative business is no more followed from Nantucket, the Quaker burying ground has memorial stones in it, and the women go to Town-Meeting and vote for School Committee, but amid all these changes, the name of Mary Starbuck, nee Coffin, is revered, as that of a wise and good woman: a trusted and honored wife, and the mother of the first, white, female child born upon the island, named like herself, MARY STARBUCK.

" Whether these Marys ever went to 'Sconset," was the querying response of the practical, as well as poetical, Helen, which was unanswered, but it was decided that if they did, they had Indians there for company, but no Continental summer visitors; plenty of fish for food,

but no bathing in the surf; the whisperings of lovers,
but no base-ball matches; moonlight rambles on the
beach, but no ice-cream saloons; plenty of house-work
to do, but no lawn-tennis or croquet, and, in fact, that
'Sconset' in those days, was not even what Mr. Flagg
calls it in his unique volume,* "a lonesome, little watering place on the extreme, eastern verge of Nantucket,
hardly anything more than a fishing village," but was the
veritable fishing village itself, and no "watering place"
at all.

But the "Siasconset influences," to use Mr. Flagg's
term, were there then, no doubt, and, as in later days,
the lover of that period could, as he says, appreciate the
loved one. Then, as now, "that required no exclusion
of other attractions, no Siasconset dullness, no con-
tracted dwellings, no narrow lanes or pathways, no wide
sea-view or sky-view ; no moon-sheen or star-sheen on
the waters at evening ; no soft zephyrs coming over the
moor-land at morning." Then, as now, perhaps it
could be said, as Mr. Flagg says: "Siasconset is not
merely ruled by softening influences, shed on it by sky
and sea and romantic moor-land, but it is a place well
contrived for throwing people together. The streets
are narrow, the paths narrow, and the rooms no larger

---

* "Wall Street and the Woods." p. 54.

than closets.   Blessed forever be proximity!"   And yet,
perhaps in Mary Starbuck's time it was only a place of
wigwams, or a place to be reached on a walk from
Sesachacha— *Quien sabe!* Yet it must always have been
a place where the weary head and heart could find rest,
leaning close to the loving heart of Nature.   The blue
skies, the far horizon, the murmuring surf, the sea-gull
dipping his wings in the dark waters, the moors with
their blossoms, the beach with its shells, the life-giving
breezes from the wide ocean, and the peculiar sense of
being so far away from the world as to be very near to
the Infinite—all these were surely there, for they make
'Sconset, and without them 'Sconset could not be.

CHAPTER XVII.

BARNACLES AND BATHERS.

"Almost a thousand years ago
　　The Norseman's venturous keel
　　Ploughed from the icy-island bays,
　　And found, for woe or weal,
　　The land we call our native isle,
　　The harbors that we know;
　　They locked upon Nantucket's shores
　　A thousand years ago."

　　　　　　　　　　　　PHEBE A. HANAFORD.

ET us walk along toward Mr. Flagg's!" was the sug-
gestive remark of the N. M., with an urging look,
and the others, smilingly—went. It was on the edge of
the bank to the north, and was reached shortly after
passing the Hamlet, known as White's, because built by
the enterprising, Detroit citizen of that uncolored name.
There was a time when the Flagg cottage crowned the
hill in stately and lonely grandeur. What a queer
edifice! some said—for it had a front-room and piazza
all in one, and its windows were made for letting in the

summer air, and closing out the winter storms, therefore
not large, nor greatly glazed.   All alone, out there, the
hospitable author and his family dwelt for a decade of
summers, more or less—alone as to houses near, not
alone as to the society of cultured and even renowned
persons.   But when the crowds of summer visitors came,
and the cottages encroached upon the dignified isolation
of the earlier discoverer of 'Sconset attractions—the
house began to be forsaken, the owners perched upon a
breezy, Connecticut hill-top in a town at once ridge and
field—and the Flagg mansion was deserted.   But when
the N. M. and her party went there, it was inhabited by
its cordial and intelligent owners.   And how pleasant
the talk of old times and of new—of the far away old
times when the Norsemen visited the Vinland of their
times and the America of ours—and of the still more
ancient days when the Parsee worshipper adored the sun
beneath the Chaldean skies.   Wit and wisdom   both
governed speech, as the little company sat on the
sheltered piazza, and looked far out over the heaving
sea.   Just in front of them bloomed the yellow cactus—
the prickly pear—which had probably been brought
thither from Coatue,* where it is indigenous, and far
off upon the sunset-tinted waves could be seen a school

---

* The northern limit of the plant on the Atlantic Coast.—M. L. Owen.

of black-fish disporting themselves, and as they passed
the village in their huge gambols, attracting the attention of all. Eyes and spy-glasses were levelled at them,
till they rolled and tumbled no more within the line of
'Sconset vision. These great sea-dwellers are often observed near the island when the smaller fishes are con-
gregated there, which become the prey of the black-fish,
and form their food. But they are seldom, or never,
caught from the shore, at present, however it may have
been in the long-ago days of the early whalers.

As the party came down from the North into the
village, there were indications of some attraction on the
beach. Groups of laughing maidens, the rush of an
occasional boy, and even a bevy of the stately matrons,
were perceived going down bank. What did it mean?
Pretty soon two or three young girls were met, each accompanied by a favorite boy-companion, and one of the
sweet-faced misses called out, " Oh, Aunties, aren't you
going on the beach to see the moon rise?" It was all
accounted for ; Emily Ruggles had revealed the secret.
The moon-rising was the event. And, on the beach, the
people, younger and older, gathered, and the songs of
that evening hour were very sweet as the villagers and
their visitors waited for the silvery light of the rising
moon to shimmer across the broad waters. At last it

came, and the stillness of watchers with it. And then
a burst of welcome! And brighter and wider gleamed
the silvery pathway from the far horizon to the shore,
as the queen of night rose toward the zenith. It was
an evening to be remembered. But it was only one of
many such in a summer at 'Sconset; beautiful to per-
ceive and enjoy, and fadelessly beautiful in the memory
thereof. The clumsy gambolling of the porpoises, the
yellow charm of the island cactus, even the pleasant
chat of ancient customs and far-off peoples, were forgotten for the while, in the always-to-be-remembered
glory of that rising moon. Such pictures stay in the
halls of memory, and there are those who watch the
seals at San Francisco, and gaze delightedly over Pacific
waters, who can close their eyes and see those pictures
hanging there forever, which make them long to cross
the Rocky Mountains, and reach 'Sconset before moon-
rise on a summer evening, that they may live over again
the exquisite enjoyment of such a well-remembered
time.

Night passed, the moon paled in the light of day,
eleven A. M. arrived, and the bathers again assembled on
the beach. Then the photographer drew nigh.

"Run, Lillian," exclaimed Helen, "you and your
cousin Phebe, run and be taken!"

No sooner said than done. Nimble feet sped over the sands, and now, in many far-scattered homes, is a picture of the bathers, watched by two little girls, in the foreground of the picture, very near the line of the surf—one, gracefully standing, "unworried" (as "Uncle Aldrich" said once) and the other drawing back, as if she feared the undertow would sweep their bare feet off the shining sands. The photograph, became an engraving of goodly size, the large engraving was reduced to a little wood-cut, and in pamphlet and paper the bathers and the two little girls are now immortalized and exhibited, far and near, and all because the quick-witted Helen impatiently shouted "Run, Lillian, run!"

"Did you see Jean on the beach to-day?" asked Helen of the N. M., "when she discovered those barnacles?"

"Not when her eyes first lighted on them, but I heard her exclaim, and rushed to share her ecstacy," was the answer.

Just then the invalid appeared in the sitting-room, with her hand full of something apparently very precious.

"Helen," she said, "these are goose-neck barnacles."

"Well, I'm not such a goosey I don't know it," was the quick reply, "I took some off the bottom of a molasses schooner, which had just come from the West Indies,

once, at a Jersey City dock, and I'm not likely to forget
how I hunted up the name of the five-shelled animal."

The N. M. smiled, and said Helen's memory was
always good—in fact, too good sometimes, when one
would like to have her forget events or words.

And then the talk floated away to the great spar or
timber, which had been thrown upon the beach at
'Sconset by some final wave, after its long journey over
the stormy deep. It was well covered. What a tale it
might have told of shipwreck and sorrow if it could
only have spoken concerning its ocean wanderings! Far
out in tropic seas it may have been wrenched from the
ship to which it belonged, and been tossed by the waves
in the vicinity of coral islands; or it may have been
part of a craft which was wrecked by contact with the
tumbling ice-berg, floating from the far North into the
very path of our fishermen and steamers. There was no
mark upon it, and no voice to tell who felled the
forest tree, and shaped the timber for the ocean voyage.
Thoughtful men and women gathered the barnacles
from it, and talked of its unknown history. And some
of them went up the bank to read that poem, sweet and
strong in its rare simplicity, written by John W. Chad-
wick, and called "My Barnacles." And as he depicts
the mollusks rejoicing over a little gift, from his hand,

of the briny sea, and reads to men a lesson of helpful-
ness, he emphasises the lesson of trust in God with his
words:

> " 'They take, with thanks, the human help,
>   And still with patience wait
> For the vast love to come and fill
>   The void it doth create.
>
> So wait our souls on Thee, O God !
>   Their longing is from Thee ;
> All human help must ever hint
>   At Thy sufficiency.
>
> Come as the ocean comes, to give
>   Its energy divine ;
> Fold us in Thy encircling arms
>   And make us wholly Thine.'

CHAPTER XVIII.

SOROSIS AT SIASCONSET.

"And when we've clasped the parting hand
   And sailed the foaming sea,
Our hearts will ever fondly turn,
   Dear, island home, to thee.
Will homeward fondly turn, dear friends,
   To school days bright and free,
Our hearts will turn, while life shall burn,
   Dear, island home, to thee."

            MRS. MARIA L. OWEN.

MONTHS passed away. The N. M. and the two sisters finished their vacation season at 'Sconset and took the wagon first, to town, and then the steamer, to the main land. Halcyon hours fly swiftly, and finally vanish as with a flash, but they leave a radiant memory. The heart of Siasconset had been revealed to them all. They had seen the natives of the village and the visitors, in seasons grave and gay, and had learned the acceptable truth that the simplicity of vacation-days at 'Sconset was in sweet accord with the kindliness of spirit

which marked personal interest ; and that the villagers
rejoiced in each other's joy, and shared in each other's
griefs, till it could be said that the heart of Siasconset
was thoroughly sympathetic, and the social influence of
the little village was of that character which was at once
uplifting and inspiring in the direction of kind words
and good works.　It seemed to be taken for granted, at
'Sconset, that the Apostle's words. were true—"God
hath made of one blood all nations for to dwell on all
the face of the earth,"—and as the solidarity of humanity was apprehended, every thoughtful soul acknowl-
edged—what the unthinking also felt—that those other
golden words for social use are true—viz.: " Love is the
fulfilling of the law."

With such impressions of the highest social attain-
ment, the N. M. one autumn found herself again at
'Sconset and a guest of the Nantucket Sorosis which had
gathered in a cottage full of precious memories ; where
many a literary star, and many a widely known philan-
thropist had spent some restful hours.　Hither to visit
the owners—Nathaniel and Eliza Barney—had often
come their honored kinswoman Lucretia Mott, with her
noble husband, James Mott:—all four being pioneers in
the philanthropic efforts which finally resulted in freedom for all persons under the American flag.

And hither on that bright, autumnal day, when the N. M. was there, came others who were also pioneers, and younger women who were happy in following in the steps of those who, long ago, led the way in paths of usefulness to paths of fame.

Linda and Sarah (dear names!) were there to represent the venerable mother whose face already wore the ethereal look of one who had done noble work on earth, and was only waiting the summons to the better land. How we longed to have her with us, for the sweet smile which always accompanied the wise words lingered in our memories, and we missed both in that social hour! But the occasion was a memorable one, and a record of it was preserved in the " Nantucket Journal " of October 1, 1885, and shall find further preservation and wider reach, perhaps, by being transferred to these pages, since all the exercises were in harmony with that social, sympathetic spirit which Helen was the first to term "the heart of Siasconset," and which phrase has become the title of this little book. Here is the newspaper report:

" On Monday, September 28, 1885, Sorosis was entertained in a most delightful manner by Mrs. H. B. Sharpe, at the residence of Mrs. Joseph S. Barney at Siasconset. Although the weather was unpropitious yet a goodly number boarded the train at 10 A. M., at the above date,

and the atmosphere soon catching the infection of sunny
smiles and happy laughter, dried up its tears, and allowed old Sol to kiss the golden rod that nodded its
good-morning to us as we sped on to the popular health-
giving resort.

Our vice-president, Mrs. Linda S. Barney, had preceded us, and upon our arrival we found the tables already spread, and only awaiting the delicious viands
which Nantucket picnic-baskets are sure to contain.
After an hour's pleasant chit-chat we were summoned
to dinner, to which ample justice was done. Anyone
who has travelled over this well-patronized road knows
its wonderful power as an appetizer.

The natural cravings appeased, our worthy president,
Miss Anna Gardner, opened the literary budget by the
following scholarly address:

"From time immemorial, from the days when the
nectarian feasts of the gods were celebrated, to this day
at Siasconset, when less ethereal and more substantial
food is served, gathering around the festive board, mingl-
ing the feast of reason with the flow of the solvent fluid,
has been the universal custom of society on occasions
like this, (a good custom where *Hygeia* is recognized as
the reigning goddess,) an ever recurring sacrament of
love and friendship. Brain and heart are reached and

nurtured through the avenues of sense. The Boston
craze, the mind cure, is based upon the subtle relations
of mind and body. This so-called new theory of thera-
peutics (old as Methuselah) widely discussed by Kant (?)
and other philosophers of the eighteenth century (minus
the fraudulent, avaricious side) contains much that is
true and beneficial to mankind. It is the 'survival of
the fittest' in the doctrines taught by Locke and Bacon
as to the identity of mind and matter. Some of us can
remember the ferment in intellectual circles caused by
such discussions fifty years ago. The physician who is
not likewise a metaphysician will be nothing fifty years
hence.

I will not detain you from the good things coming,
but simply bespeak a pleasant time for all, and say with
Shakspeare, 'may good digestion wait on appetite, and
health on both.'"

Mrs. Hannah M. Robinson read the following original
poem, descriptive of the difficulties attending the finding
of the meaning of the word "Sorosis:"

"Sorosis! what is it and where doth it dwell?
To what kingdom belong? Can any one tell?
Did it first greet the morn where the stars had their birth?
Or has it more recently beamed upon earth?
Does it dwell in the breezes, the perfumes of flowers?
And sport with the elves through the long, sunny hours?

Is its murmur as soft as the twitter of doves,
Or the brook's whisper low to the flowers that it loves?
Does it compass us round 'mid our labors and cares,
Like the angel of verse entertained unawares?
Or is it something that's tangible, visible, real,
Helping ignorance and vice to a higher ideal?
I have gone back to Noah (Noah Webster, I mean)
To see if the least ray of light I could glean
Of the word with a meaning so exceedingly ambiguous.
Alas, 'twas not there, nor anything contiguous—
To Worcester and Johnson I vainly appealed
Their lips, alias leaves, were hermetically sealed.
Did I give up the quest?—'twould be something uncommon
For ignorance to win when its foe was a woman.
For some time I sat in deep meditation,
As if not alone my fate but that of the nation
Depended on this problem's rapid solution;
It was evidently the offspring of some evolution
Of which I was ignorant—very easy you say,
For my philosophy, like Horatio's, to be deficient that way;
But my resolve had been taken and earth, sea, and sky
Should list to my queries till I gained a reply.
So forth to the woods I sallied at morn,
When the black veil of night from our earth had been torn,
And the birds and the flowers and the insects that creep,
Were bathing in sunshine—only mortals could sleep;
There I shouted and shouted, ' Who to ignorance a foe is,
Come forth and tell me, oh! what is Sorosis?'
I listened and heard in the trees such a chatter
Of monkeys, as saying, ' Pray what is the matter?'

Of all our dear Darwinian brothers who have come here to declaim,
Not one have we heard pronounce that queer name.
The trees shook their heads and the birds flew away,
And I not a whit wiser for questioning that day ;
To the breast of old Ocean I carried my moan,
But naught could I hear save the deep undertone
Of that orchestra grand, deep down in the waves,
Where the mermaids trip light in their own coral caves;
Crest-fallen—not vanquished—I stood 'neath the stars,
With my one single question—commencing with Mars ;
But he put on his armour as if for a fight,
And I quickly withdrew, I think wisely, from sight :
The Great Bear only growled at being disturbed,
And in fact the whole heavens seemed greatly perturbed.
Several stars, I'll not name them, ran off with the dipper,
And from the course that they took, I fear, for a nipper,
And who'd blame them if while watching this isle of the sea
They saw God's image was licensed, and said, " why not we ?"
So potent is example—'tis a lesson for all,
That not alone may we rise, nor alone must we fall.
The moon 'neath a cloud hid her sad, serious face,
As if she especially felt the disgrace
Of ignorance in the Queen of Night's brilliant daughter,
You'd have thought from her countenance she had lost her last
        quarter.
More in pity than anger my steps homeward turned,
Each defeat adding fuel to the fire that now burned
So fierce in my brain, it absorbed my existence
To such an extent I defied all resistance.

Find the meaning I would, let it cost what it may,
And I did, patient listener, after many a day;
The Trades I assailed, hoping there I might find
Some solution that would serve as panacea to my mind;
The cobbler couldn't tell me in detail, but as a whole,
He believed it related to the immorta'ity of the *soul:*
The farmer declared that he was just *beat;*
But he'd *turn-up* the earth from one to four feet
In hopes 'twas a mineral full eighteen *carrots* fine
Which he'd *cabbage* and *call-it-a-flower* most divine.
The merchant declared it grew not in the earth,
But was some article of toilet imported from Worth.
Which idea the dressmaker *flounced* as absurd,
I saw her opinion was *biased*, and referred
To the tailor at once—he declared it not *suit*-ed
To his style of thought; he panted for knowledge
And would give it some heed, but since he left college
He'd done little else than grow out of knowledge,
But added with zeal "I really *trow, sir*,
We shall very soon know more than what we do now, sir."
The M. D., so versed in pills and in blisters,
Said he'd heard 'twas a club they called "Sorry Sisters."
(How changed his opinion if he were but able,
To glance at the faces convened round this table.)
But his idea of a club, perhaps he was right,
And though it took me all summer, on this line I would fight.
Be patient, dear listener, my tale is soon done.
I'll not recount battles lost, or name victories won
Time passed, and once more my feet trod the soil
Of my own native isle, whose air is like oil

On the tempest-tost waves to the thousands who seek
Repose for the weary, and rest for the weak ;
'Mong others an infant was brought to our shores
By its god-mother Morse (all know her of course)
It was sent by its mother for our island's adoption
Far away from the din of the city's corruption,
Its features were winsome, and we could do no other
Than give it a welcome, we so loved its god-mother.
I asked, "What's your name? Pray tell, if you know, sis."
Imagine my surprise when she answered "Sorosis!"
And this is our club which we tenderly nurse,   •
About which we write doggerel (it can't be called verse.)
For this hour's amusement ; judge not of our aim,
Or think this the style in which we usually declaim.
In more serious moments we sing a new song
Of justice and right, 'gainst injustice and wrong.
Our heart's aspirations ascend to the True,
We discard old ideas and welcome the new ;
We claim close relation to all that is human,
And inscribe on our banner—"The Elevation of Woman!"

Miss Mabel Sharpe, read, with much effect, a sweet, little song called "The Golden Rod."

Mrs. Charlotte A. Joy Mann read, in her usual clear and distinct voice, so pleasant to the ear, an article entitled "The Shadow of the Harem," by T. W. Higginson.

Mrs. H. B. Sharpe read Victor Hugo's "Credo," to the gratification of all present.

Mr. S. H. Mann read a brief article by James Parton.
The President gave the following original article as a
sort of supplement to " Childe Harold's Pilgrimage," the
Childe terminating his pilgrimage at 'Sconset:

Stretching afar along the shelving bank,
  Behold a village by the sounding sea —
Dwellings in groups, or standing rank on rank,
  A novel aspect to the stranger's ee.
The marvel grows, and gazing wonderingly,
Childe Harold views the antiquated sights,
  The unique signs on cottage, fence and tree,
From White's trim hamlet, on to Sunset Heights.
What flaunting image now upon his vision lights,

While treading narrow lanes by dwellings quaint?
  A fancy figure tall, Dame Gossip said,
A certain skipper, brave, (though not a saint)
  Modelled this form from one he'd fain have wed,
  When, in his youth a seaman's life he led ;
And many other views the Childe could see,
  And annals hear, on which his fancy fed,
Of whilom 'Sconset manners, easy, free—
Then idly gazing, lo, what queerity !

The sign " Utopia !" Fabled land of rest !
  The Childe had travelled many a weary year
And little thought that island of the blest
  In this forsaken region would appear,
  Bringing his journey to an end so near.

What is that central figure, old and gray?
  The village pump! you read its title clear,
Hence to that trysting place he wends his way
To quench his ardent thirst—his curiosity.

Shades of the past! Fain would he something learn
  Of this strange people, this sequestered place.
To the Post-office then his footsteps turn—
  Some wight may there instruct him how to trace
  Through guarled roots this simple-hearted race,
Deeming what men call *progress* simply *loss*,
  For ancient landmarks they would ne'er efface.
Rushing and snorting comes the iron horse,
An innovation strange which they do not endorse.

Back to the Beacon-light he bends his way,
  The fame whereof had reached him long before,
He wanders on the heights of Sankoty,
  And listens to the ocean's wildest roar,
  Whose billows chafe and foam along the shore
Then turns to gaze upon a landscape rare,
  Calming his being to its inmost care—
On undulating hills and vales, that wear
Robes of the deepest green, bedecked with flowers fair.

Wide spreads the prospect on to Pocomo,
  And to Saul's Hills that glimmer in the light,
With evening sunbeams they are all aglow—
  Where could a fairer prospect meet the sight,
  Or charm the spirit of an anchorite?

One with the soul of Nature—blending free,
  Inspired and lifted by its subtle might,
Childe Harold drew from halls of memory
An innovation sweet—his own apostrophe.

"Dear Nature is the kindest mother still,
  Though always changing in her aspect mild;
From her bare bosom let me take my fill,
  Her never weaned, though not her favored, child.
  Oh! she is fairest in her features wild,
Where nothing polished dares pollute her path;
  To me, by day or night, she ever smiled,
Though I have marked her when no other hath,
And sought her more and more, and loved her best in wrath."

To 'Sconset back he slowly wends his way,
  As lengthening shadows show the day's decline,
The village people, whether grave or gay
  Again to meet, and never to resign
  The new found life from which to press the wine
Of sweet content—of cheerfulness and joy,
  Nor ever for the world beyond to pine—
Quaffing the cup which does not swiftly cloy,
  Where happiness is found without its deep alloy.

With a view of calling out Rev. P. A. Hanaford, Mrs.
Sarah S. Swain read a poem by that lady, entitled "The
Right Marching On."

THE RIGHT MARCHING ON.

Our hearts are weary, waiting for the coming of the day,
When the barriers of progress are forever moved away ;
When the women, as the men, shall the ballot-scepter sway,
         And Right go marching on.

In the front of every battle still we see the holy souls,
Whom the law of righteous freedom, only, evermore controls,
And whose women, as whose men, should be equal at the polls,
         That Right go marching on.

Our eyes are lifted upward to the chariots of fire,
That are bearing from among us, to the blessed angel-choir,
Some whose gospel song of freedom soundeth clearer now and
      higher,
         As Right goes marching on.

We miss them in the forum, and we miss them in the field—
Souls of strength and grace and wisdom that to Wrong could never
      yield,
In whose lives the life of heaven is forever more revealed,
         As Right goes marching on.

In their footsteps we move onward to the glory of the height,
Where they wait the victor-anthems telling triumphs of the Right,
With a vision cleared of error in the day that has no night,
         While Right goes marching on.

In the conflict weary not, then, for the victory is ours ;
For the bow of promise shineth after all the vanished showers,
And the fruit is folded surely in the petals of the flowers,
         As Right goes marching on.

Mrs. Hanaford responded promptly, and concluded her remarks by the following original article:

SOROSIS AT SIASCONSET.

We gather in gladness, we gather in hope,
  For the dawn hath appeared, and the day;
No longer in darkness the spirit may grope,
  But we walk in the Truth's divine ray.

We have learned that the path of the just groweth bright,
  And that justice means freedom and peace,
That from man unto man, and to woman each right
  Must be given ere darkness will cease.

Yes, the day-star has paled with the glory of morn,
  The bright beams of the day-god appear,
And the flag which some high souls so bravely have borne
  Tells the eagles of victory near.

Now woman and man, side by side, may engage
  In the help of world and its toil,
And the strife which for equal rights ever is waged
  Finds an end on American soil.

Sorosis gives welcome to Truth and to Right
  Where 'Sconset laws must be obeyed,
And the faces of friends are as gleamings of light
  From the land where no blossom shall fade.

From Sorosis the mother, to this island child
　Comes greeting your course to approve;
May the years, as they go and come, find undefiled
　The fame of this child of our love.

Success to the efforts which still may be made,
　In the line of advancement by you!
Success to the banner you're bearing aloft!
　Success to the brave and the true!

Rev. Louise S. Baker was then called, and in the course of her pertinent remarks made a very happy allusion to the sentiment expressed in the stanzas of the "Golden Rod."

Mrs. Elizabeth Starbuck contributed the following brief, original poem, as a "Summer Farewell," and, later, addressed toasts to most of those present, which from their local and personal significance were highly enjoyed by the recipients.

SUMMER FAREWELL.

We gather to-day when the rich glow of sunset
　Illumines our path with its halo of light;
When the sighing of winds, and the moaning of ocean,
　Combine in their echoes the voices of night.

In splendor and glory, with magical fleetness,
　The summer has come, and the summer has gone,
Like the glance of a sunbeam in beauty and sweetness,
　That peers through the clouds, and then passes on.

The day's programme came to a happy termination by the singing of the following, written by Mrs. Sarah B. Willetts for the occasion.

Come let us join our voices
In song before we go ;
Old Ocean's waves will catch the strain,
And bear it as they flow.
And when we meet in other years,
And other pleasures know,
We'll sing the praise of 'Sconset days—
Of 'Sconset long ago.

CHORUS.

Of 'Sconset long ago we'll sing—
Of 'Sconset long ago.
We'll sing the praise of 'Sconset days—
Of 'Sconset long ago.

Where on this bank in days of yore
The red man drew his bow,
We gather round this social board,
Cheered by wit's brightest flow,
And when with reminiscences
Our hearts are all aglow,
We'll sing, with praise, of 'Sconset days—
Of 'Sconset long ago.

CHORUS.

Had this been Adam's Paradise
  Six thousand years ago,
No tempter would have entered in
  To fill this world with woe.
Eve would have sung her vesper hymn
  In cadence sweet and low,
As we sing now of 'Sconset days,
  Of 'Sconset long ago.

CHORUS.

Now on the threshold of the night,
  Sol, lingering, bids us go,
And leave this home for water sprites
  And mermaids from below,
But let no dulling touch of time,
  When wandering to and fro,
Banish the thought of 'Sconset days—
  Of 'Sconset long ago.

CHORUS.

Thus endeth the newspaper report.

And when the pleasant hours came to an end, the
N. M. went back to Coffyn Cottage, bade farewell to
the dear ones there, and rode to Nantucket town over
the flowery plain, as driver for the President of the
Nantucket Sorosis, and her sister Sarah, worthy daugh-

ters of two of the truest abolitionists that ever sighed over the lot of the slave, or toiled for the freedom of humanity.

Nantucket has had many pioneers among its natives. The first who protested against "the oppressed Africans, in New England," was Elihu Coleman, a Quaker minister, whose book was written a hundred years before the N. M. was born, and he was an ancestor, or ancestral relative, of Prof. Maria Mitchell, LL.D., the first woman in America to engage in astronomical pursuits, and win merited distinction. Nantucket has also had many authors, both in prose and verse, among its natives, whose books have had extended circulation, and salutary influence. And, in connection with useful and wonderful inventions, scientific and geographical discoveries, and with important mercantile enterprises, the names of her children and grandchildren will be found; to an extent surprising to all those who are unacquainted with her unique people and remarkable history. Space fails the author here to tell of those who, in science, art, literature, commerce, patriotism, philanthropy, theology and reform, have themselves occupied distinguished positions, and opened doors of opportunity to others. Some future day may see that pleasant task accomplished.

Suffice it, now, to add the earnest desire that the fame

of Nantucket may never grow less, through any failure on the part of its inhabitants to imitate the virtues of the early settlers, or any lack of opportunity to display to visitors from the world over the blue waters, the genuine hospitality, the kindly sympathy, the intelligent good will, which have combined to constitute

THE HEART OF SIASCONSET.